POKÉMON™

BLACK AND WHITE

VOL.16

Story by **HIDENORI KUSAKA**
Art by **SATOSHI YAMAMOTO**

Pokémon Black and White
Volume 16
Perfect Square Edition

Story by HIDENORI KUSAKA
Art by SATOSHI YAMAMOTO

© 2014 Pokémon.
© 1995–2014 Nintendo/Creatures Inc./GAME FREAK inc.
TM, ®, and character names are trademarks of Nintendo.
POCKET MONSTERS SPECIAL (Magazine Edition)
by Hidenori KUSAKA, Satoshi YAMAMOTO
© 1997 Hidenori KUSAKA, Satoshi YAMAMOTO
All rights reserved.
Original Japanese edition published by SHOGAKUKAN.
English translation rights in the United States of America, Canada, the United Kingdom,
Ireland, Australia and New Zealand arranged with SHOGAKUKAN.

English Adaptation / Bryant Turnage
Translation / Tetsuichiro Miyaki
Touch-up & Lettering / Susan Daigle-Leach
Cover Art Assistance / Miguel Riebman
Design / Fawn Lau
Editor / Annette Roman

Printed in the U.S.A.

Published by VIZ Media, LLC
P.O. Box 77010
San Francisco, CA 94107

10 9 8 7 6 5 4 3 2 1
First printing, June 2014

www.perfectsquare.com

www.viz.com

Pokémon™

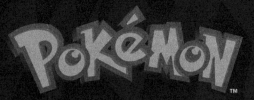

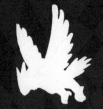

BLACK AND WHITE

VOL. 16

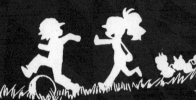

THE STORY THUS FAR!

Pokémon Trainer Black is exploring the mysterious Unova region with his brand-new Pokédex. Pokémon Trainer White runs a thriving talent agency for performing Pokémon. While traveling together, their paths cross with Team Plasma, a nefarious group that advocates releasing your Pokémon into the wild! Now Black and White are off on their own separate journeys of discovery...

BLACK'S dream is to win the Pokémon League!

WHITE'S dream is to work in show biz... and now she's learning how to Pokémon Battle as well!

Black's Munna, MUSHA, helps him think clearly by temporarily "eating" his dream.

White's Tepig, GIGI, and Black's Emboar, BO, get along like peanut butter and jelly! But Gigi left White for another Trainer...

Adventure 52
A Wretched Reunion

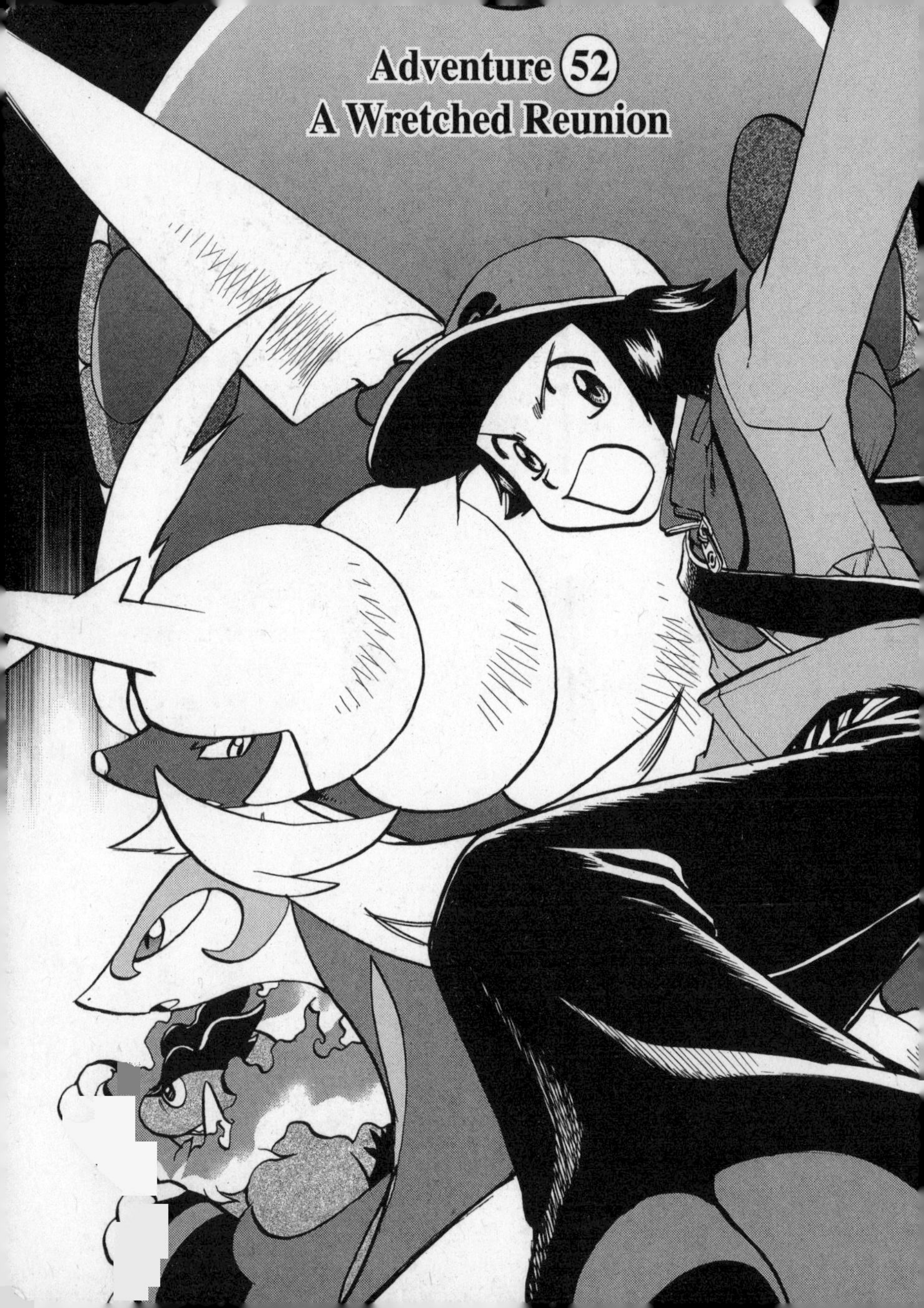

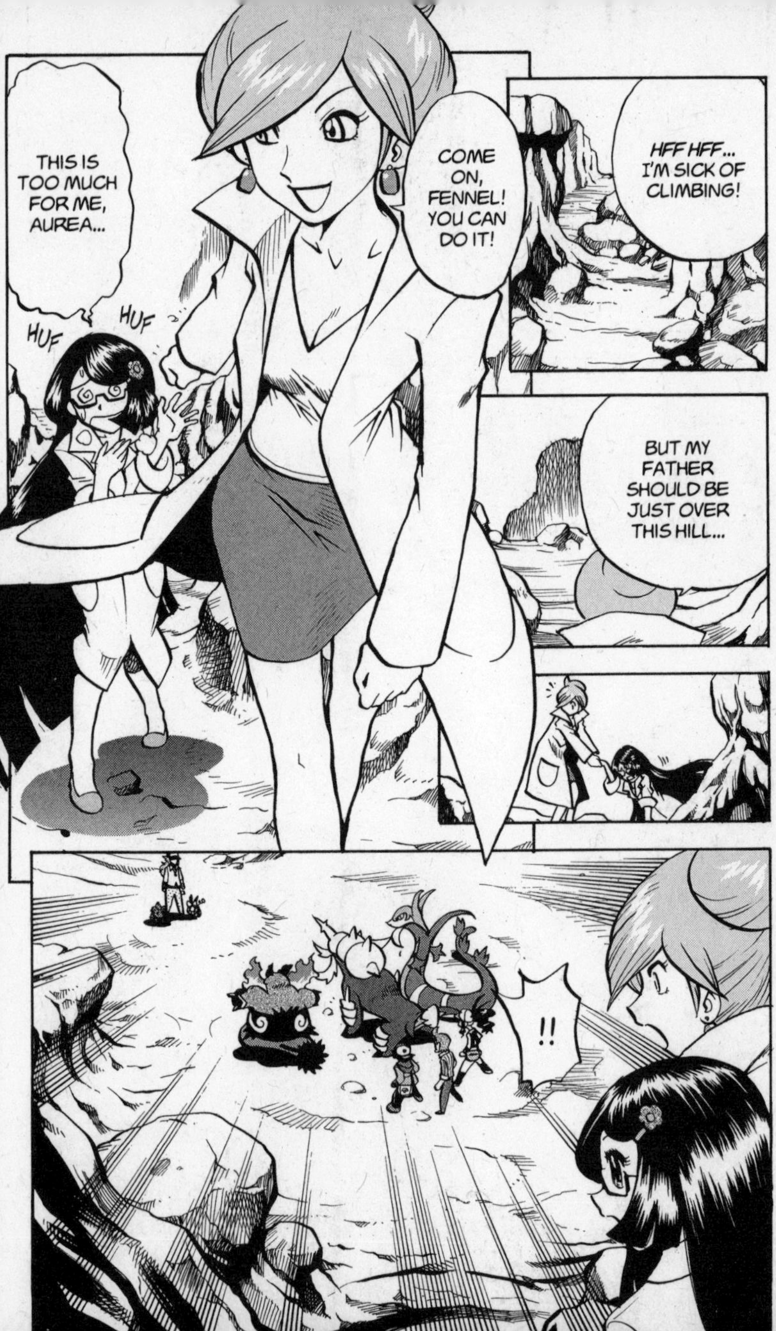
HFF HFF... I'M SICK OF CLIMBING!
BUT MY FATHER SHOULD BE JUST OVER THIS HILL...
COME ON, FENNEL! YOU CAN DO IT!
THIS IS TOO MUCH FOR ME, AUREA...
HUF
HUF
!!

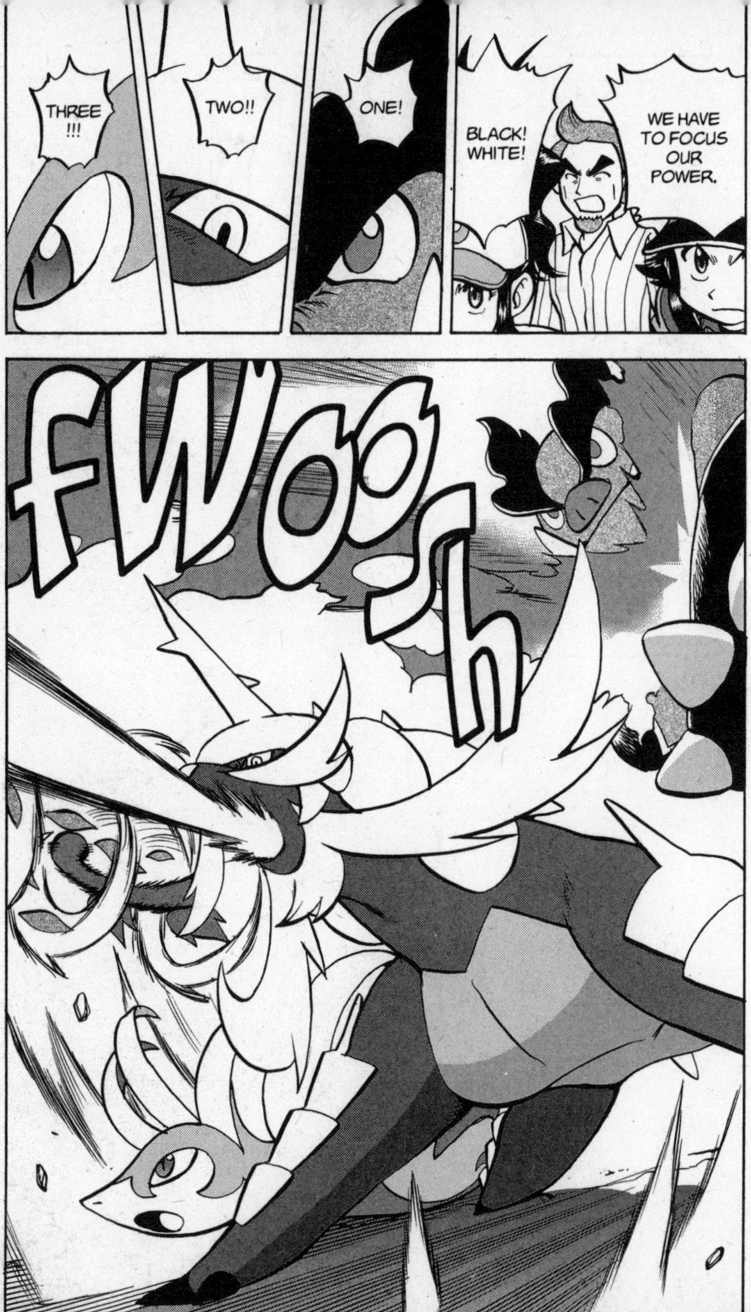
WE HAVE TO FOCUS OUR POWER.
BLACK! WHITE!
ONE!
TWO!!
THREE !!!
fWOosh

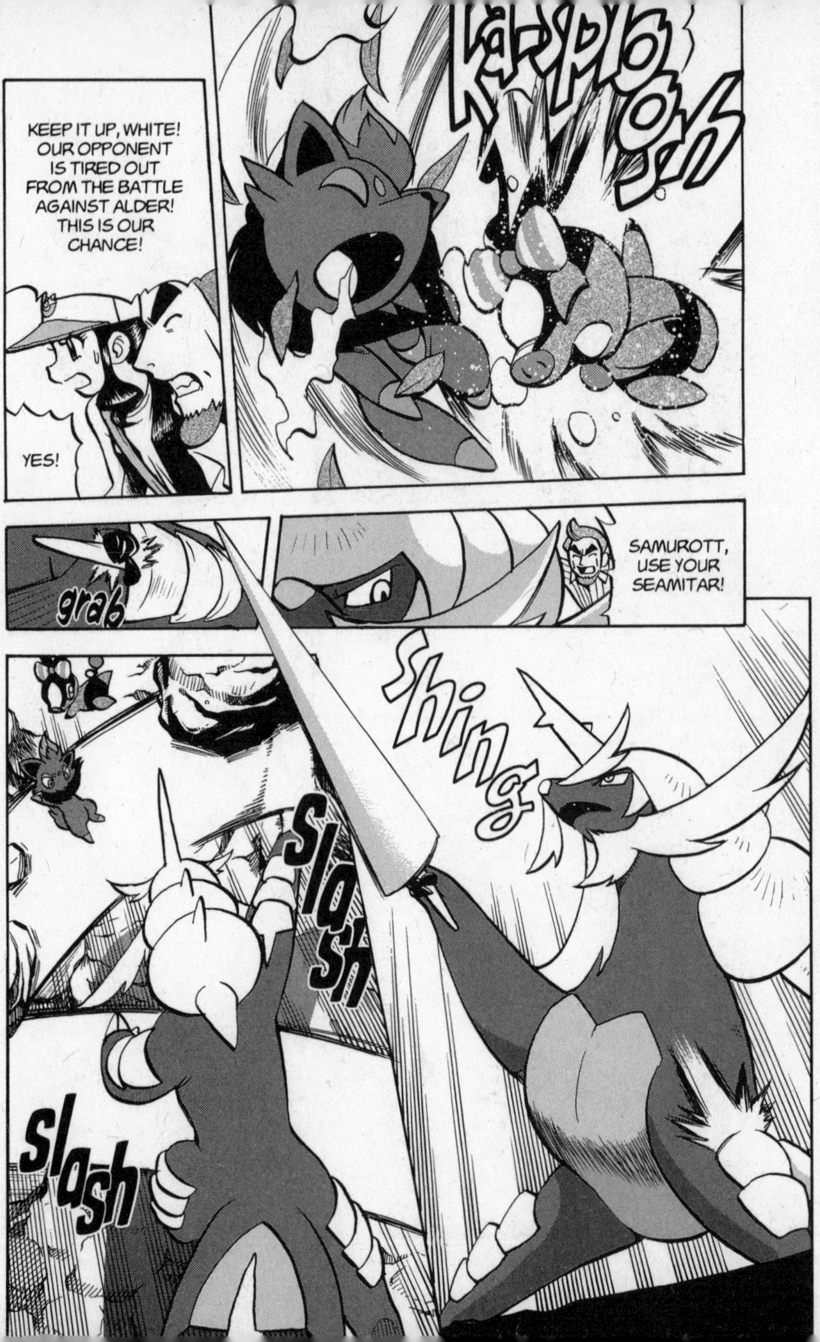

kaploosh
KEEP IT UP, WHITE! OUR OPPONENT IS TIRED OUT FROM THE BATTLE AGAINST ALDER! THIS IS OUR CHANCE!
YES!
SAMUROTT, USE YOUR SEAMITAR!
grab
shing
slash
slash

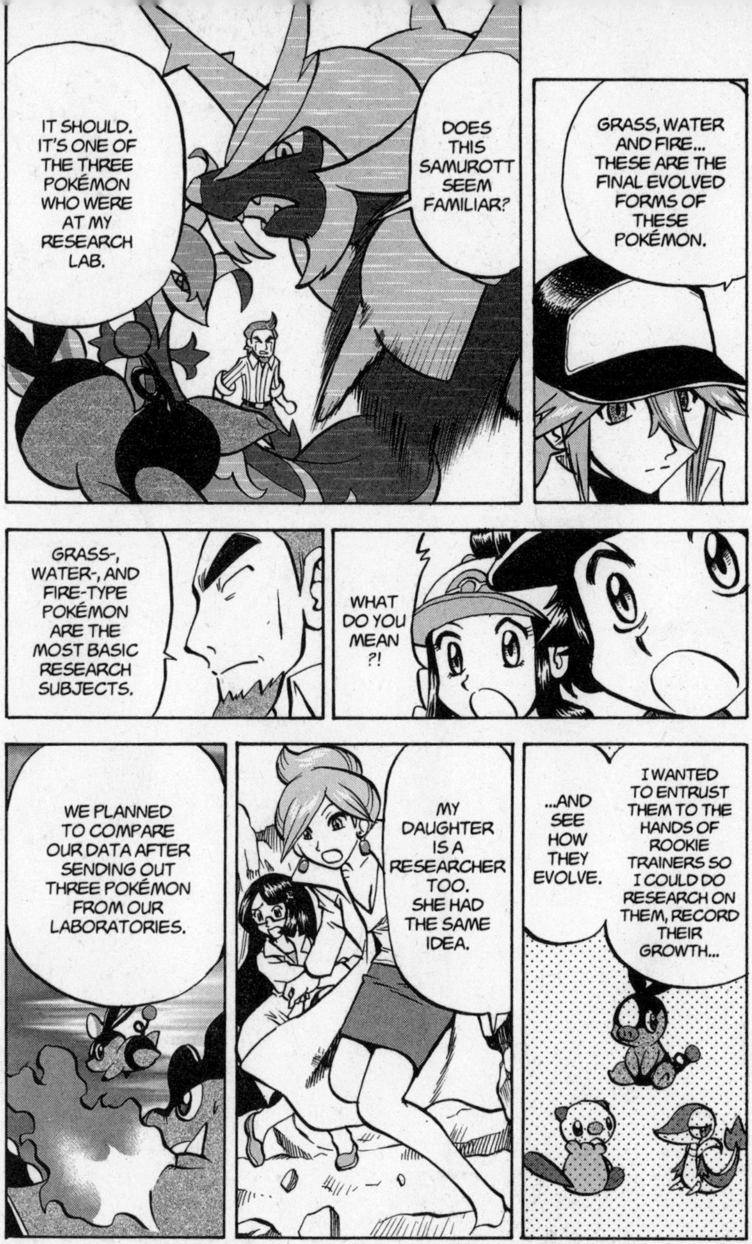
GRASS, WATER AND FIRE... THESE ARE THE FINAL EVOLVED FORMS OF THESE POKÉMON.
DOES THIS SAMUROTT SEEM FAMILIAR?
IT SHOULD. IT'S ONE OF THE THREE POKÉMON WHO WERE AT MY RESEARCH LAB.
WHAT DO YOU MEAN ?!
GRASS-, WATER-, AND FIRE-TYPE POKÉMON ARE THE MOST BASIC RESEARCH SUBJECTS.
I WANTED TO ENTRUST THEM TO THE HANDS OF ROOKIE TRAINERS SO I COULD DO RESEARCH ON THEM, RECORD THEIR GROWTH...
...AND SEE HOW THEY EVOLVE.
MY DAUGHTER IS A RESEARCHER TOO. SHE HAD THE SAME IDEA.
WE PLANNED TO COMPARE OUR DATA AFTER SENDING OUT THREE POKÉMON FROM OUR LABORATORIES.

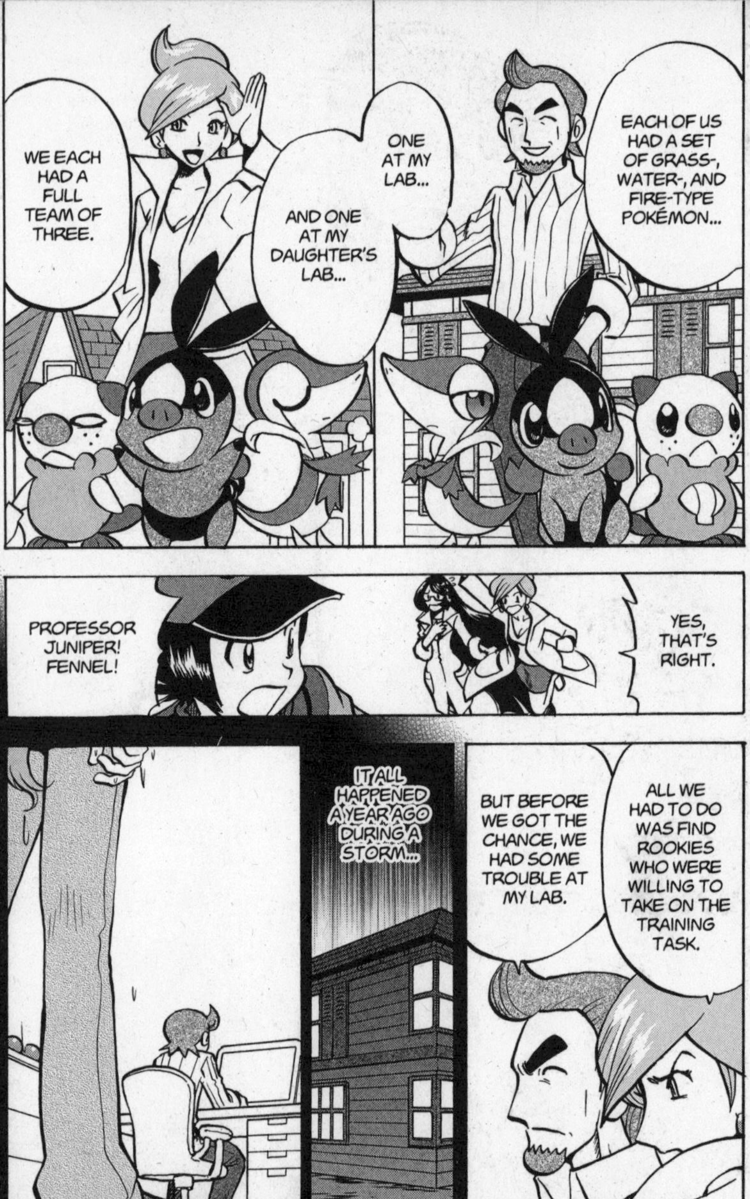
EACH OF US HAD A SET OF GRASS-, WATER-, AND FIRE-TYPE POKÉMON...
ONE AT MY LAB...
AND ONE AT MY DAUGHTER'S LAB...
WE EACH HAD A FULL TEAM OF THREE.
YES, THAT'S RIGHT.
PROFESSOR JUNIPER! FENNEL!
ALL WE HAD TO DO WAS FIND ROOKIES WHO WERE WILLING TO TAKE ON THE TRAINING TASK.
BUT BEFORE WE GOT THE CHANCE, WE HAD SOME TROUBLE AT MY LAB.
IT ALL HAPPENED A YEAR AGO DURING A STORM...

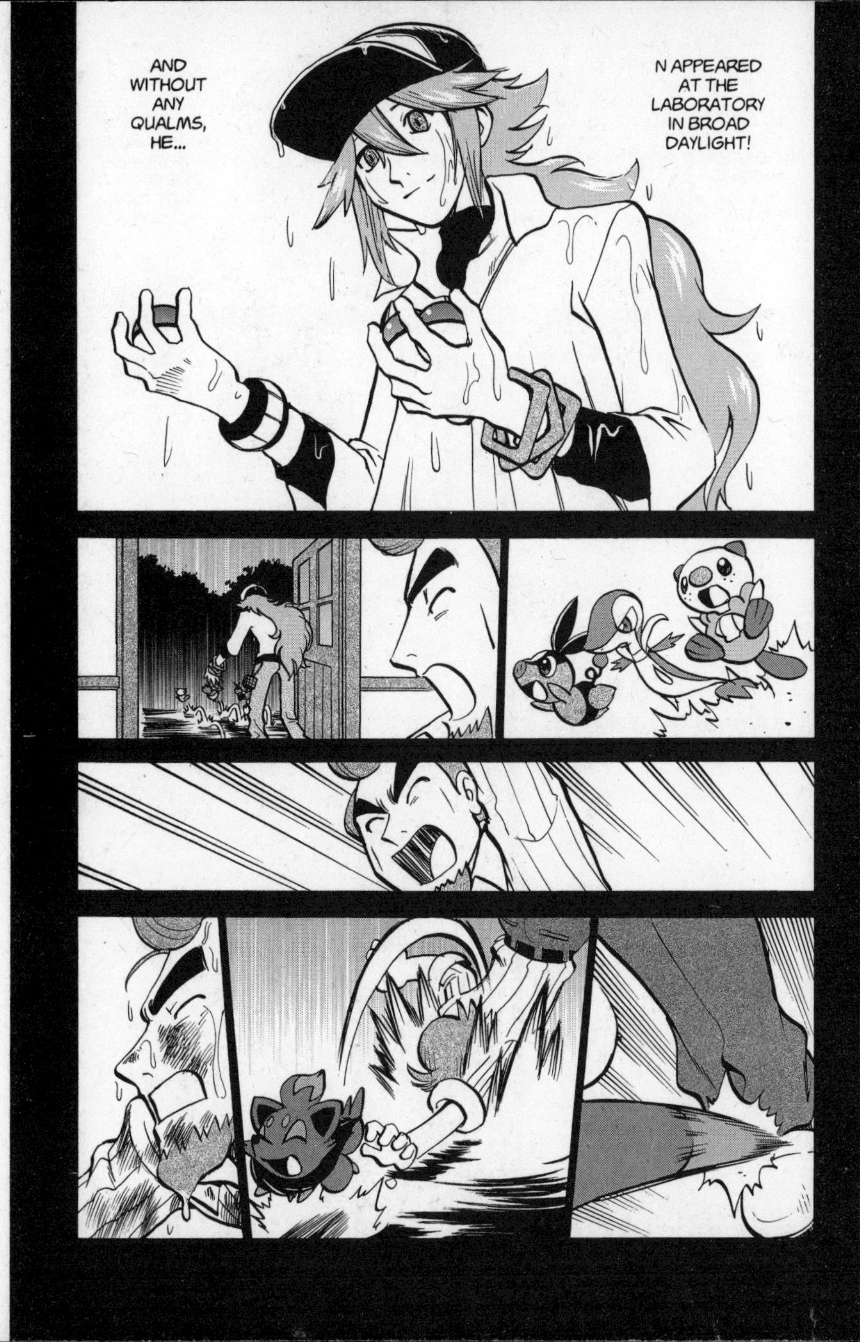
N APPEARED AT THE LABORATORY IN BROAD DAYLIGHT!
AND WITHOUT ANY QUALMS, HE...

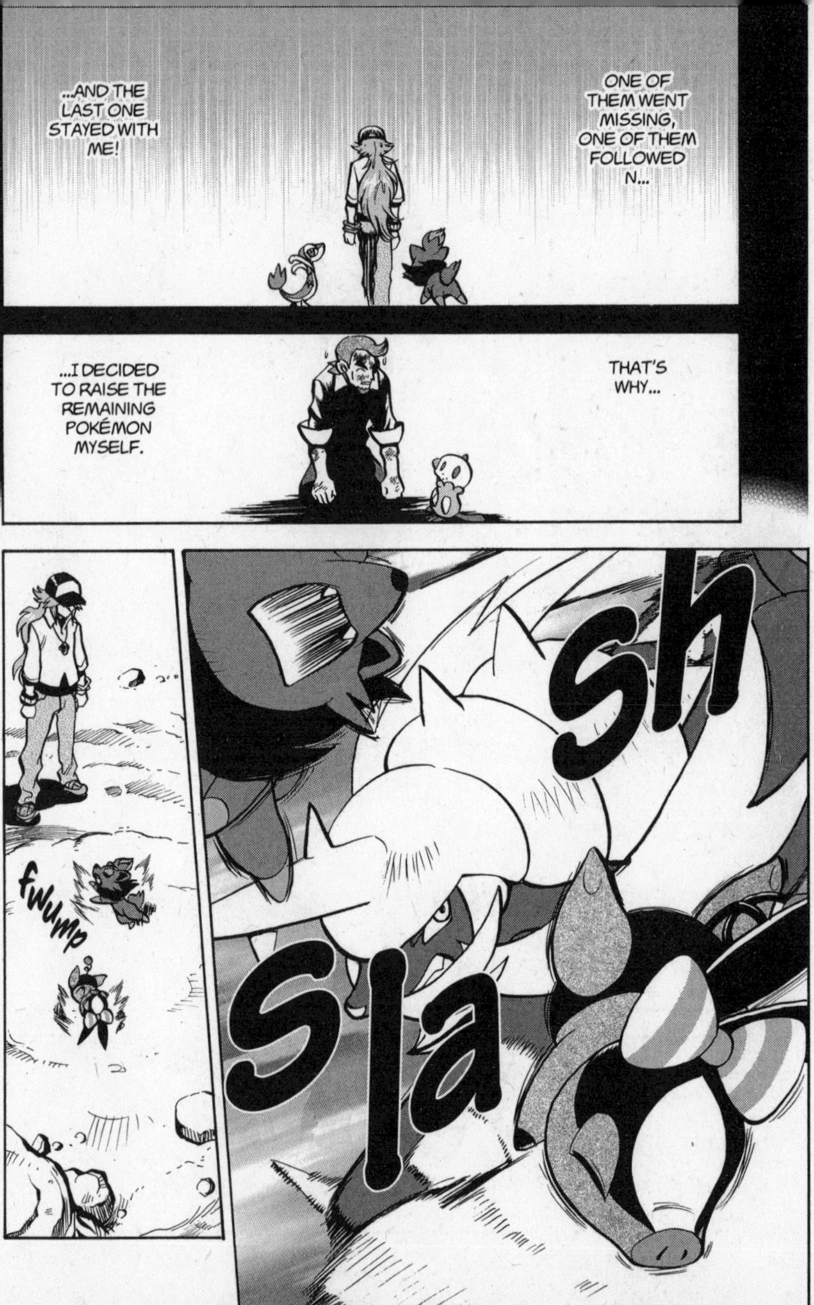
ONE OF THEM WENT MISSING, ONE OF THEM FOLLOWED N...
...AND THE LAST ONE STAYED WITH ME!
THAT'S WHY...
...I DECIDED TO RAISE THE REMAINING POKÉMON MYSELF.
Slash
fwump

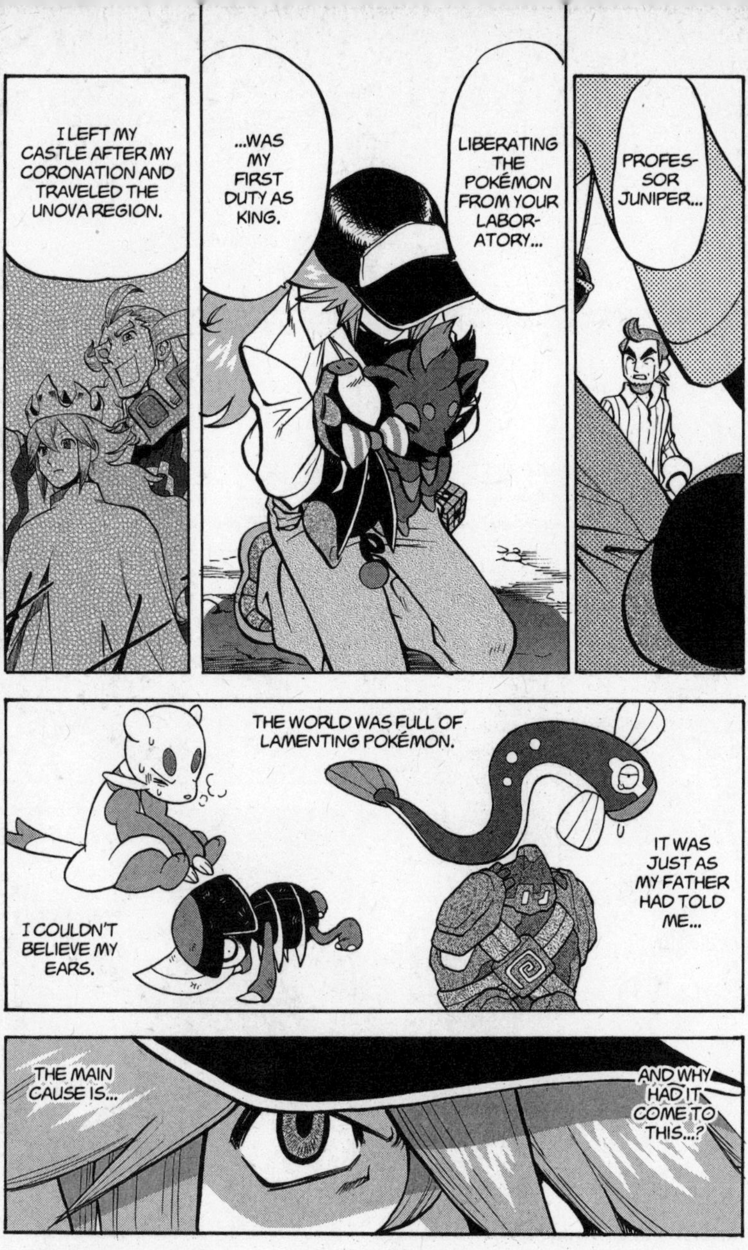
PROFESSOR JUNIPER...
LIBERATING THE POKÉMON FROM YOUR LABORATORY...
...WAS MY FIRST DUTY AS KING.
I LEFT MY CASTLE AFTER MY CORONATION AND TRAVELED THE UNOVA REGION.
THE WORLD WAS FULL OF LAMENTING POKÉMON.
IT WAS JUST AS MY FATHER HAD TOLD ME...
I COULDN'T BELIEVE MY EARS.
AND WHY HAD IT COME TO THIS...?
THE MAIN CAUSE IS...

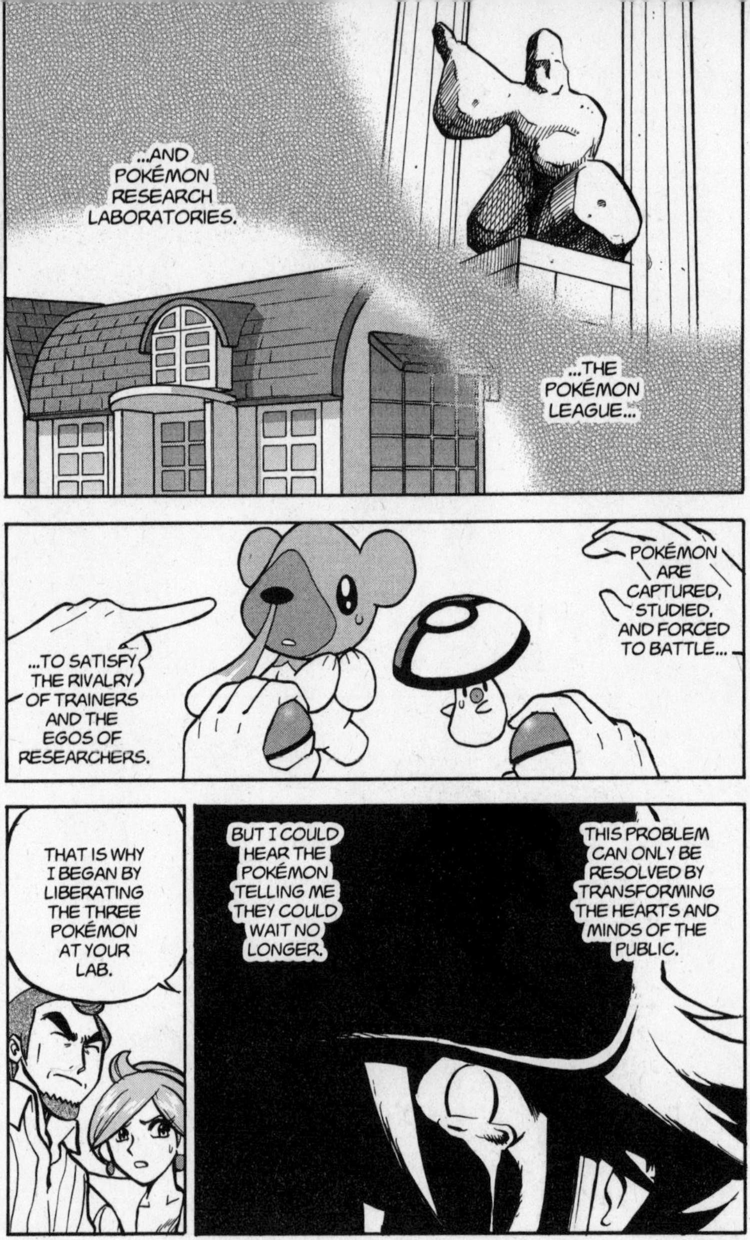
...THE POKÉMON LEAGUE...
...AND POKÉMON RESEARCH LABORATORIES.
POKÉMON ARE CAPTURED, STUDIED, AND FORCED TO BATTLE...
...TO SATISFY THE RIVALRY OF TRAINERS AND THE EGOS OF RESEARCHERS.
THIS PROBLEM CAN ONLY BE RESOLVED BY TRANSFORMING THE HEARTS AND MINDS OF THE PUBLIC.
BUT I COULD HEAR THE POKÉMON TELLING ME THEY COULD WAIT NO LONGER.
THAT IS WHY I BEGAN BY LIBERATING THE THREE POKÉMON AT YOUR LAB.

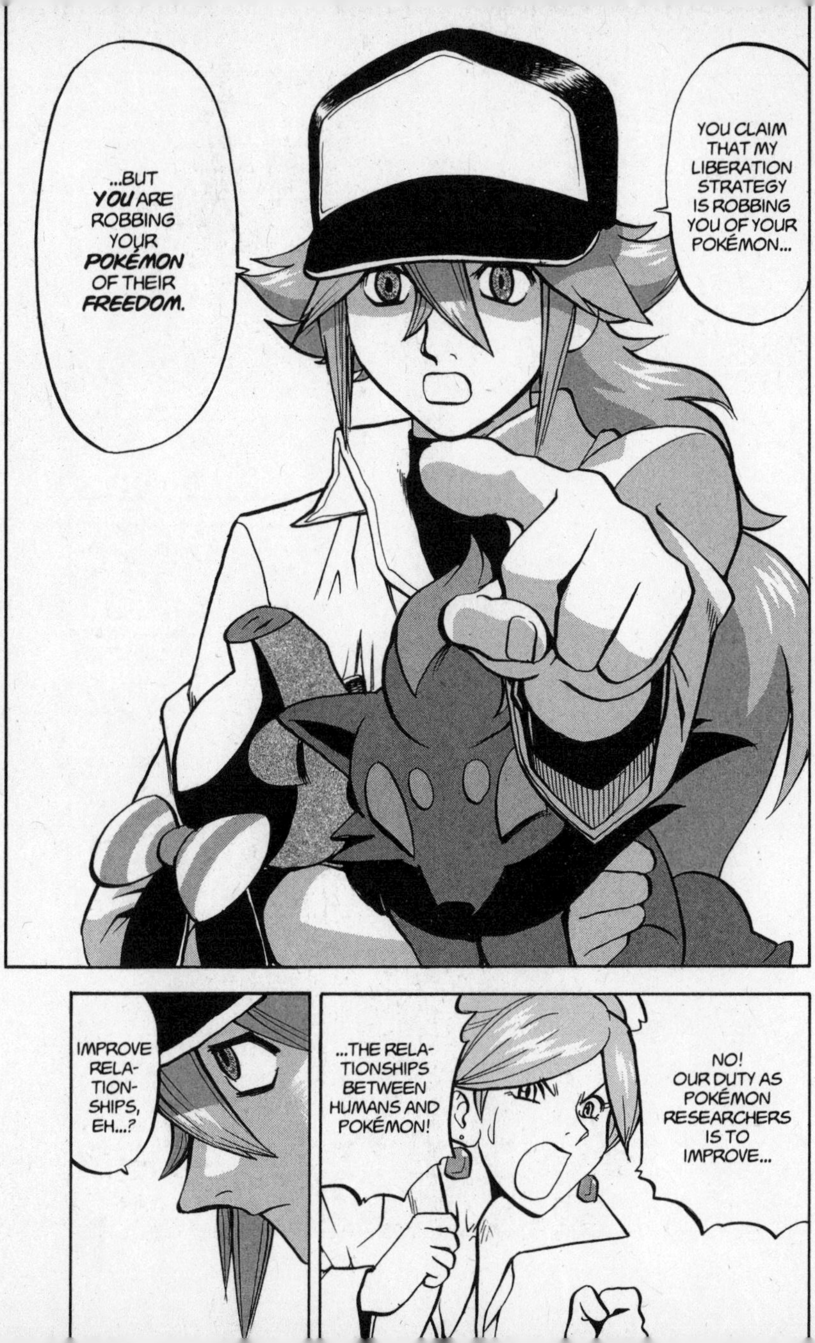
YOU CLAIM THAT MY LIBERATION STRATEGY IS ROBBING YOU OF YOUR POKÉMON...
...BUT ***YOU*** ARE ROBBING YOUR ***POKÉMON*** OF THEIR ***FREEDOM.***
NO! OUR DUTY AS POKÉMON RESEARCHERS IS TO IMPROVE...
...THE RELATIONSHIPS BETWEEN HUMANS AND POKÉMON!
IMPROVE RELATIONSHIPS, EH...?

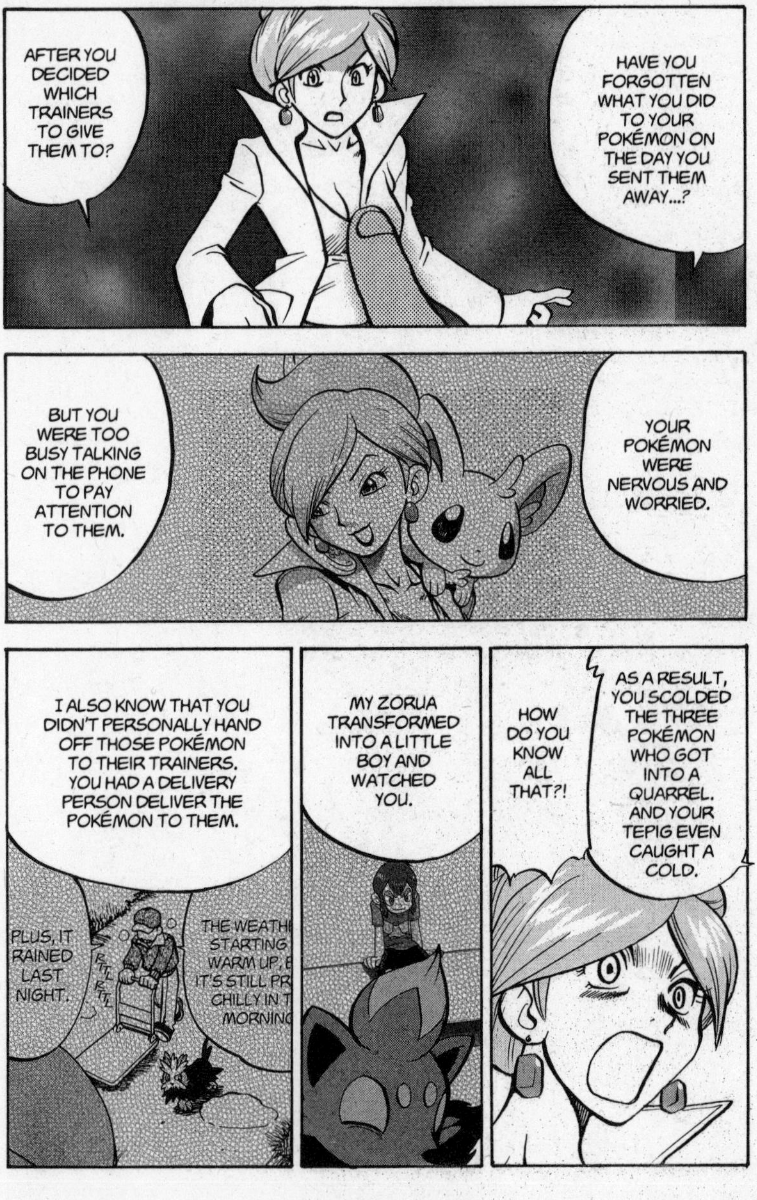
HAVE YOU FORGOTTEN WHAT YOU DID TO YOUR POKÉMON ON THE DAY YOU SENT THEM AWAY...?
AFTER YOU DECIDED WHICH TRAINERS TO GIVE THEM TO?
YOUR POKÉMON WERE NERVOUS AND WORRIED.
BUT YOU WERE TOO BUSY TALKING ON THE PHONE TO PAY ATTENTION TO THEM.
AS A RESULT, YOU SCOLDED THE THREE POKÉMON WHO GOT INTO A QUARREL. AND YOUR TEPIG EVEN CAUGHT A COLD.
HOW DO YOU KNOW ALL THAT?!
MY ZORUA TRANSFORMED INTO A LITTLE BOY AND WATCHED YOU.
I ALSO KNOW THAT YOU DIDN'T PERSONALLY HAND OFF THOSE POKÉMON TO THEIR TRAINERS. YOU HAD A DELIVERY PERSON DELIVER THE POKÉMON TO THEM.
RTTL RTTL
PLUS, IT RAINED LAST NIGHT.

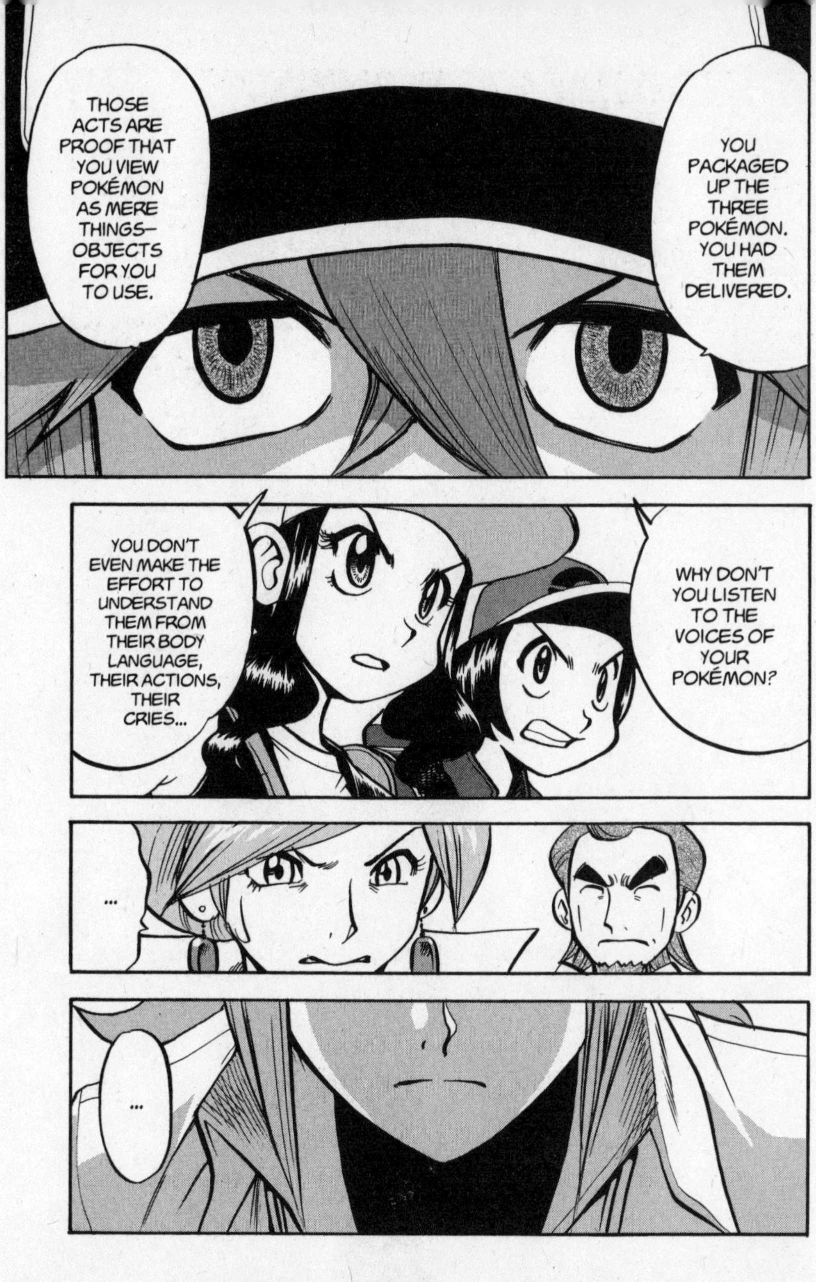
YOU PACKAGED UP THE THREE POKÉMON. YOU HAD THEM DELIVERED.
THOSE ACTS ARE PROOF THAT YOU VIEW POKÉMON AS MERE THINGS—OBJECTS FOR YOU TO USE.
WHY DON'T YOU LISTEN TO THE VOICES OF YOUR POKÉMON?
YOU DON'T EVEN MAKE THE EFFORT TO UNDERSTAND THEM FROM THEIR BODY LANGUAGE, THEIR ACTIONS, THEIR CRIES...
...
...

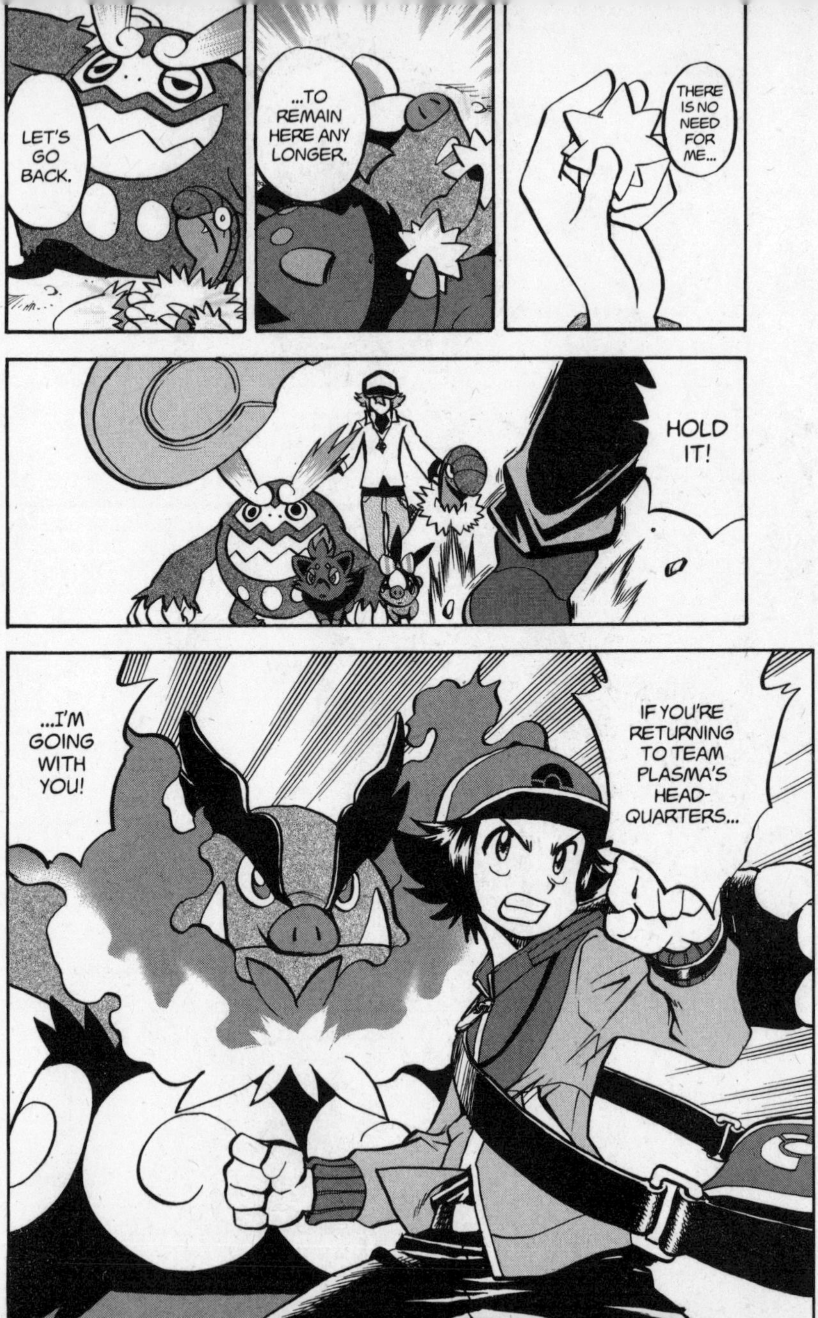
THERE IS NO NEED FOR ME...
...TO REMAIN HERE ANY LONGER.
LET'S GO BACK.
HOLD IT!
IF YOU'RE RETURNING TO TEAM PLASMA'S HEAD-QUARTERS...
...I'M GOING WITH YOU!

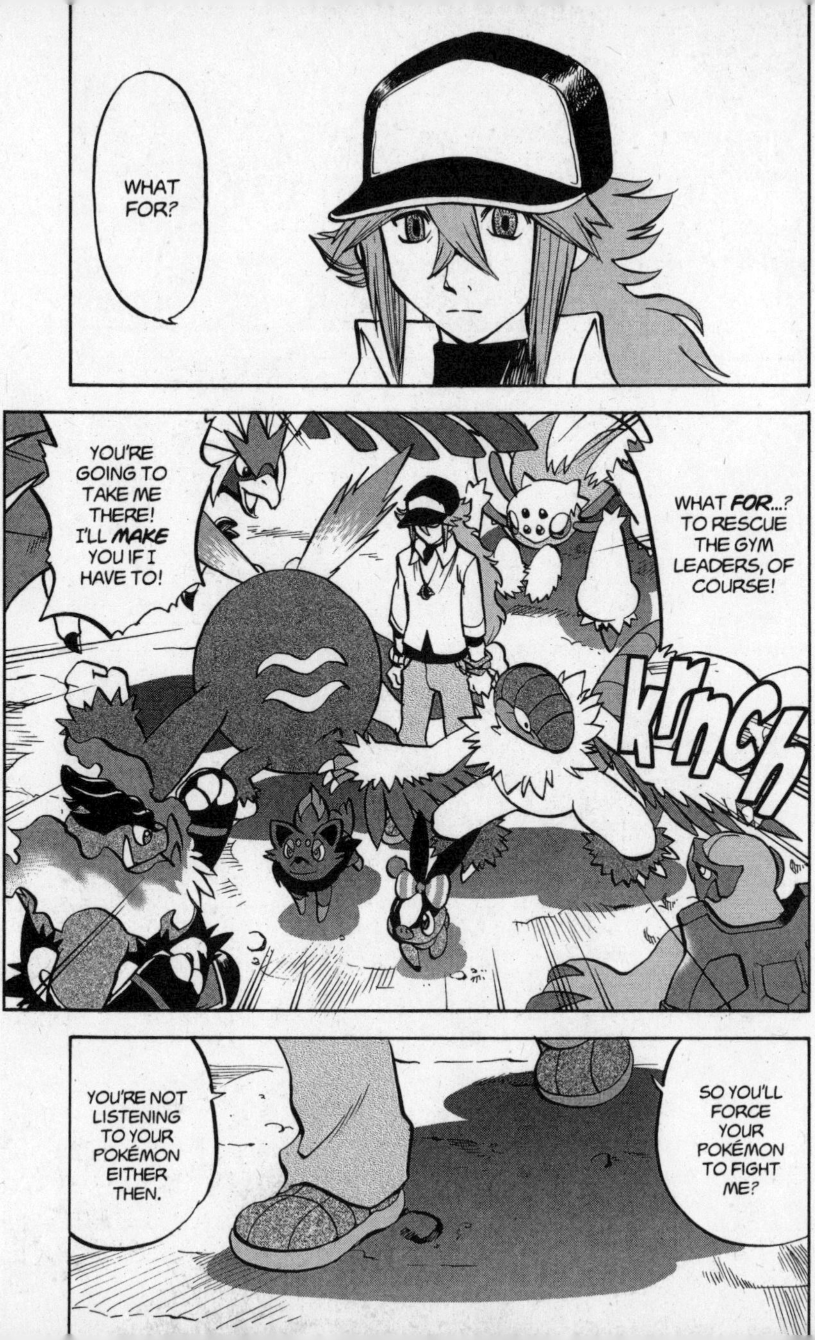
WHAT FOR?
WHAT **FOR**...? TO RESCUE THE GYM LEADERS, OF COURSE!
KRNCH
YOU'RE GOING TO TAKE ME THERE! I'LL **MAKE** YOU IF I HAVE TO!
SO YOU'LL FORCE YOUR POKÉMON TO FIGHT ME?
YOU'RE NOT LISTENING TO YOUR POKÉMON EITHER THEN.

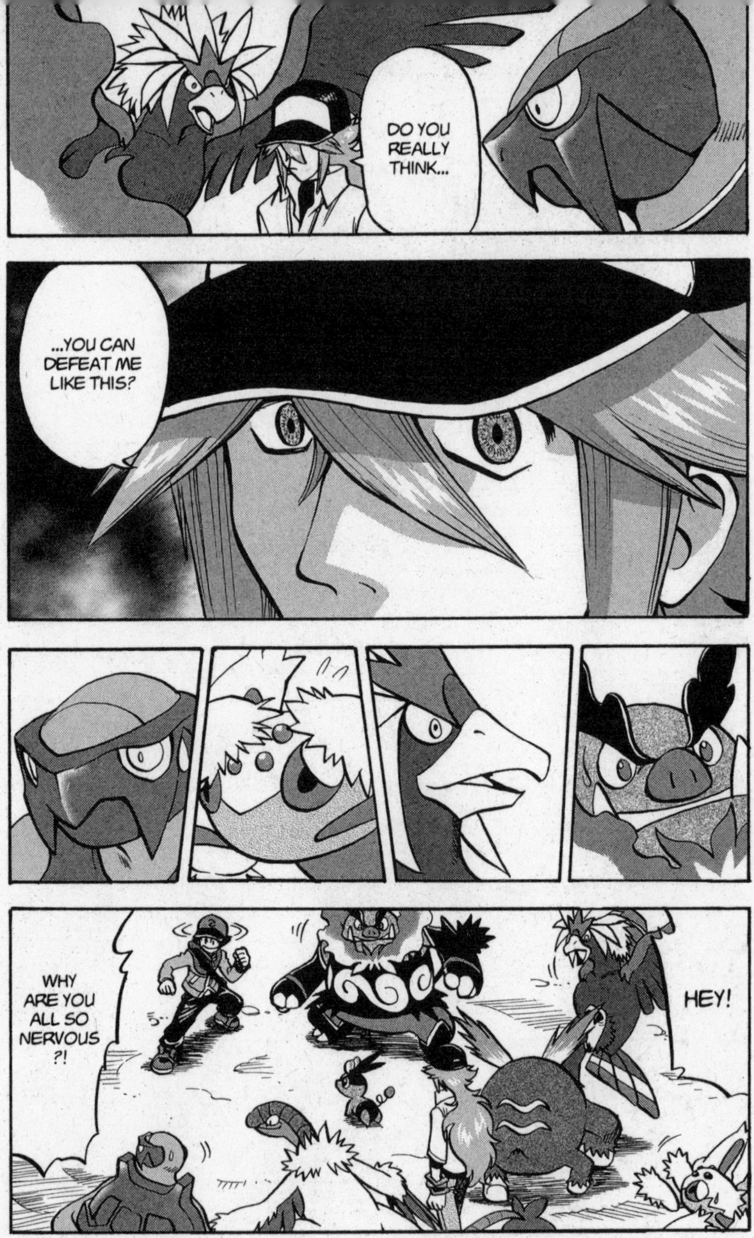
DO YOU REALLY THINK...
...YOU CAN DEFEAT ME LIKE THIS?
HEY!
WHY ARE YOU ALL SO NERVOUS ?!

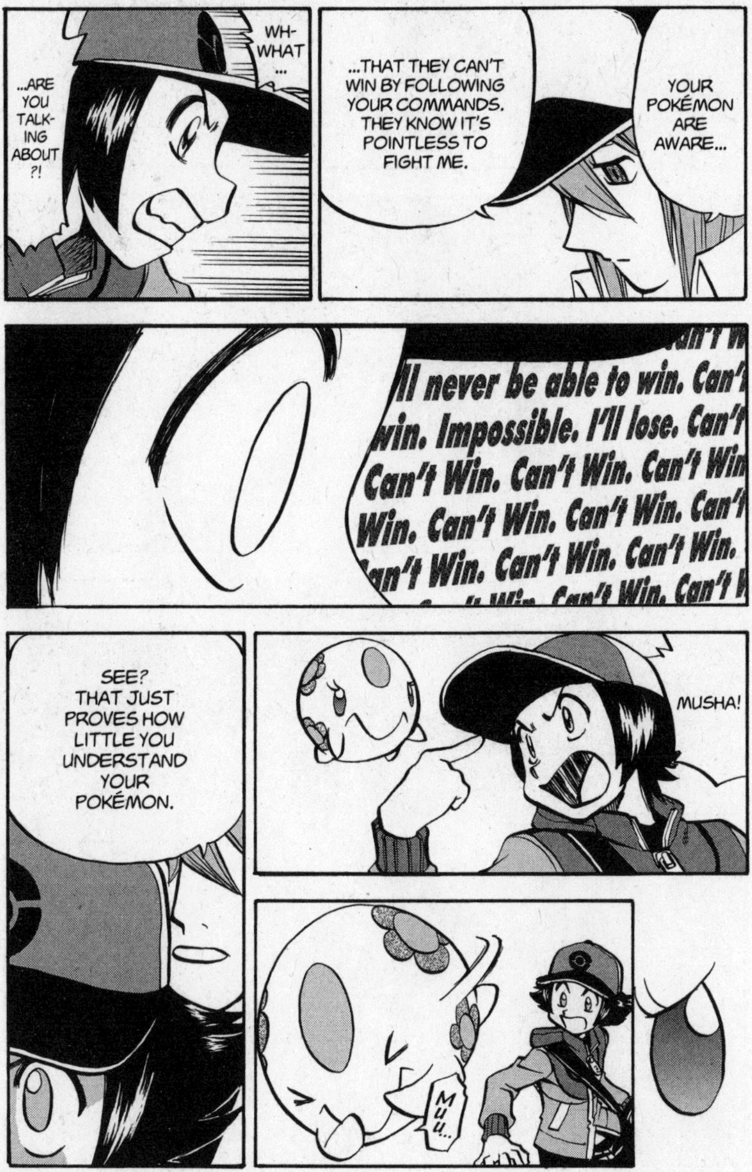
YOUR POKÉMON ARE AWARE...
...THAT THEY CAN'T WIN BY FOLLOWING YOUR COMMANDS. THEY KNOW IT'S POINTLESS TO FIGHT ME.
WH-WHAT ...
...ARE YOU TALK-ING ABOUT ?!
ll never be able to win. Can't
win. Impossible. I'll lose. Can't
Can't Win. Can't Win. Can't Win
Win. Can't Win. Can't Win. Can't
an't Win. Can't Win. Can't Win.
MUSHA!
MUU...
SEE? THAT JUST PROVES HOW LITTLE YOU UNDERSTAND YOUR POKÉMON.

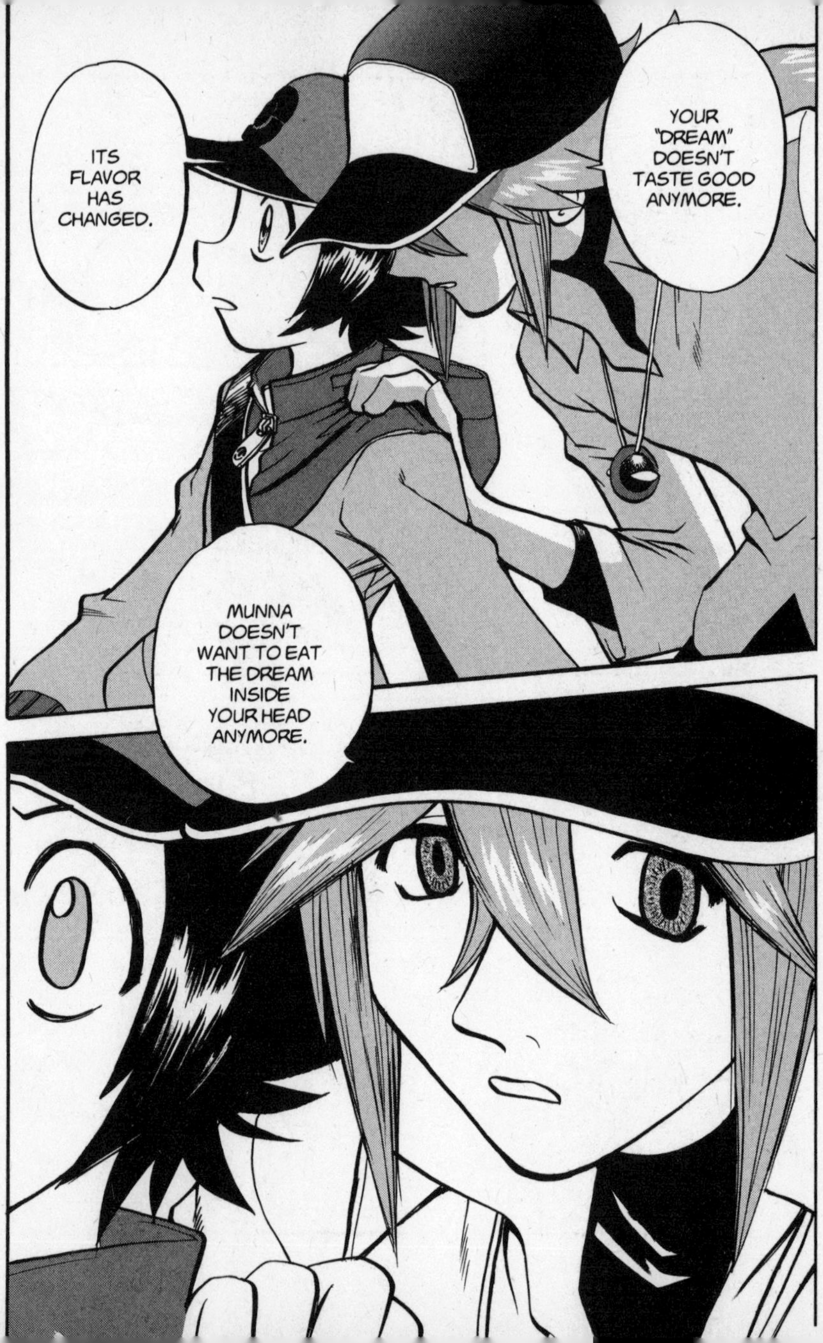
YOUR "DREAM" DOESN'T TASTE GOOD ANYMORE.
ITS FLAVOR HAS CHANGED.
MUNNA DOESN'T WANT TO EAT THE DREAM INSIDE YOUR HEAD ANYMORE.

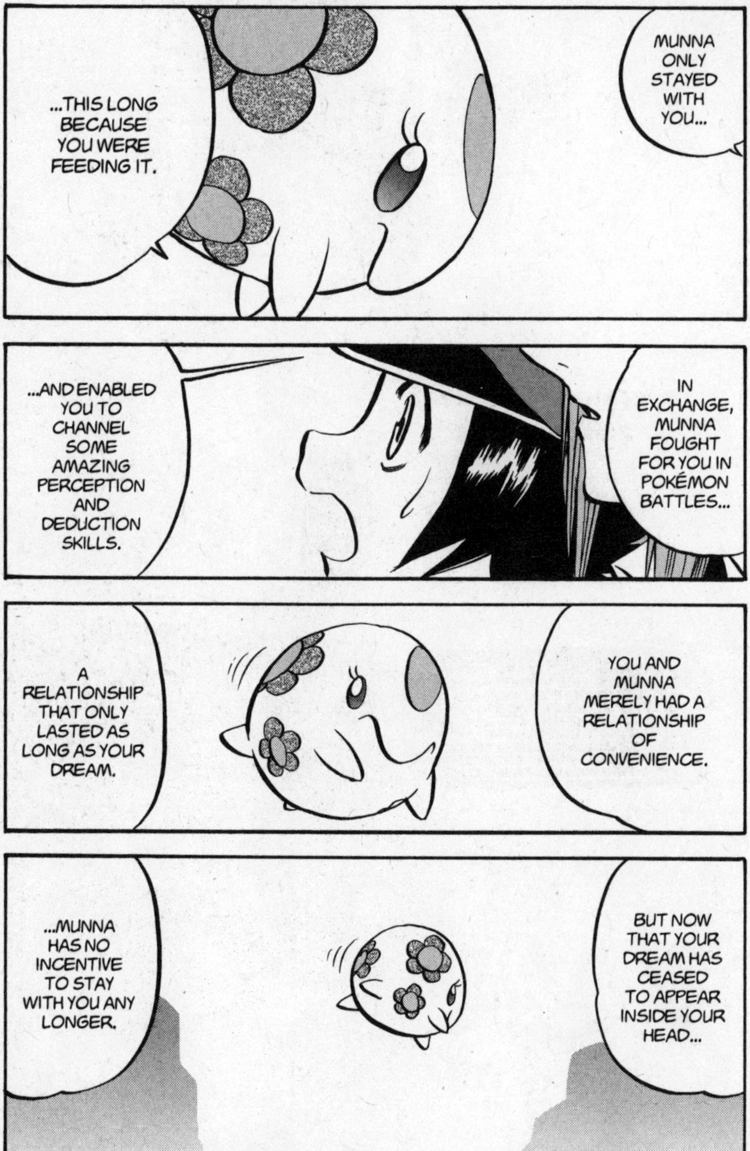
MUNNA ONLY STAYED WITH YOU...
...THIS LONG BECAUSE YOU WERE FEEDING IT.
IN EXCHANGE, MUNNA FOUGHT FOR YOU IN POKÉMON BATTLES...
...AND ENABLED YOU TO CHANNEL SOME AMAZING PERCEPTION AND DEDUCTION SKILLS.
YOU AND MUNNA MERELY HAD A RELATIONSHIP OF CONVENIENCE.
A RELATIONSHIP THAT ONLY LASTED AS LONG AS YOUR DREAM.
BUT NOW THAT YOUR DREAM HAS CEASED TO APPEAR INSIDE YOUR HEAD...
...MUNNA HAS NO INCENTIVE TO STAY WITH YOU ANY LONGER.

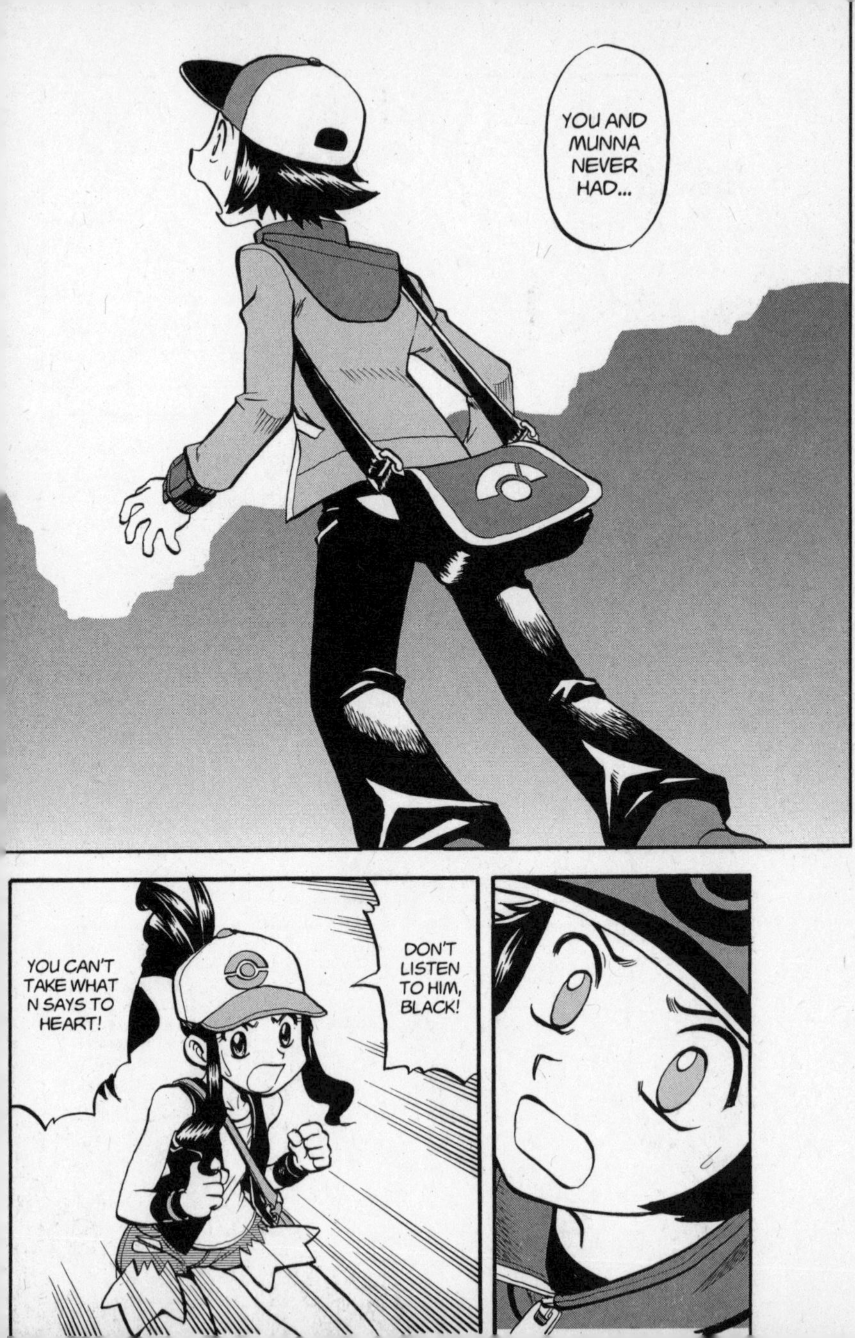
YOU AND MUNNA NEVER HAD...
DON'T LISTEN TO HIM, BLACK!
YOU CAN'T TAKE WHAT N SAYS TO HEART!

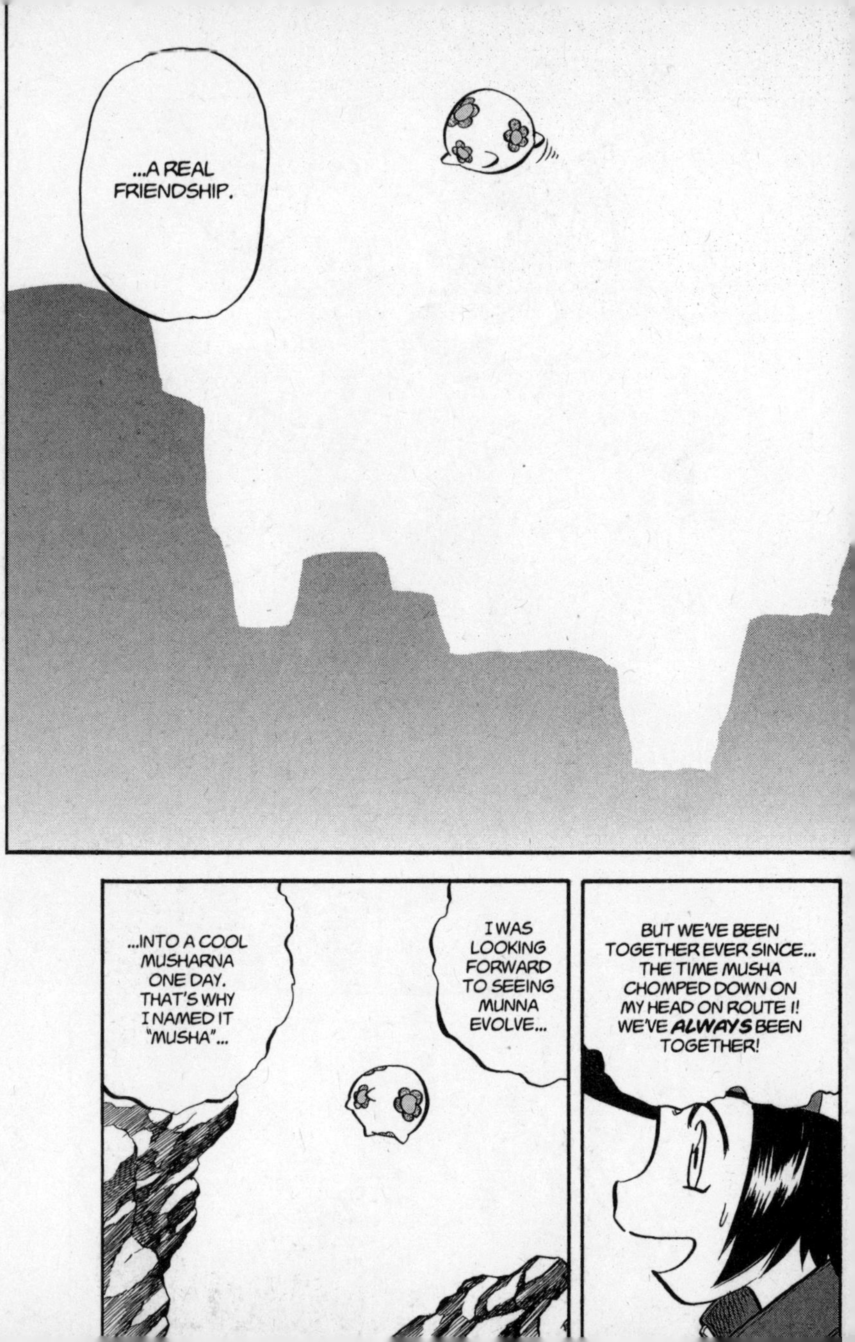
...A REAL FRIENDSHIP.
BUT WE'VE BEEN TOGETHER EVER SINCE... THE TIME MUSHA CHOMPED DOWN ON MY HEAD ON ROUTE 1! WE'VE **ALWAYS** BEEN TOGETHER!
I WAS LOOKING FORWARD TO SEEING MUNNA EVOLVE...
...INTO A COOL MUSHARNA ONE DAY. THAT'S WHY I NAMED IT "MUSHA"...

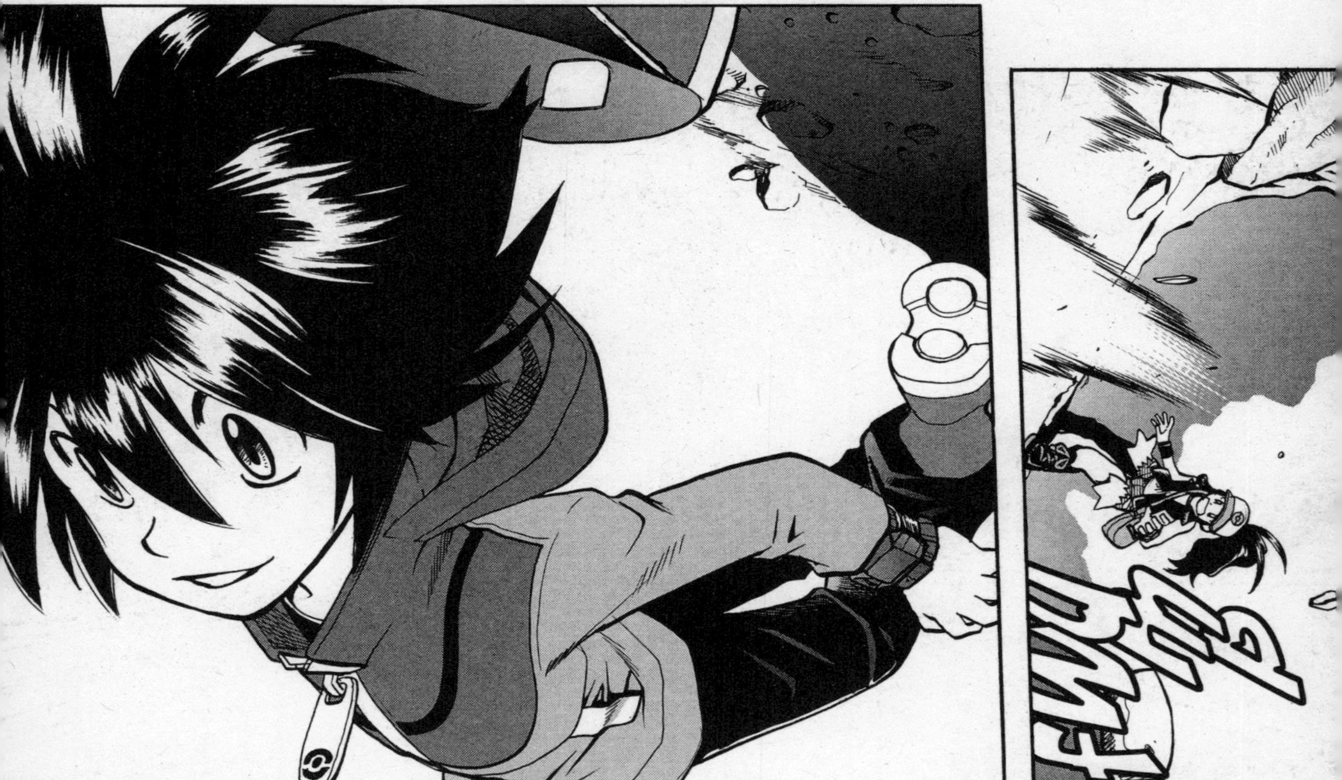
FWUMP

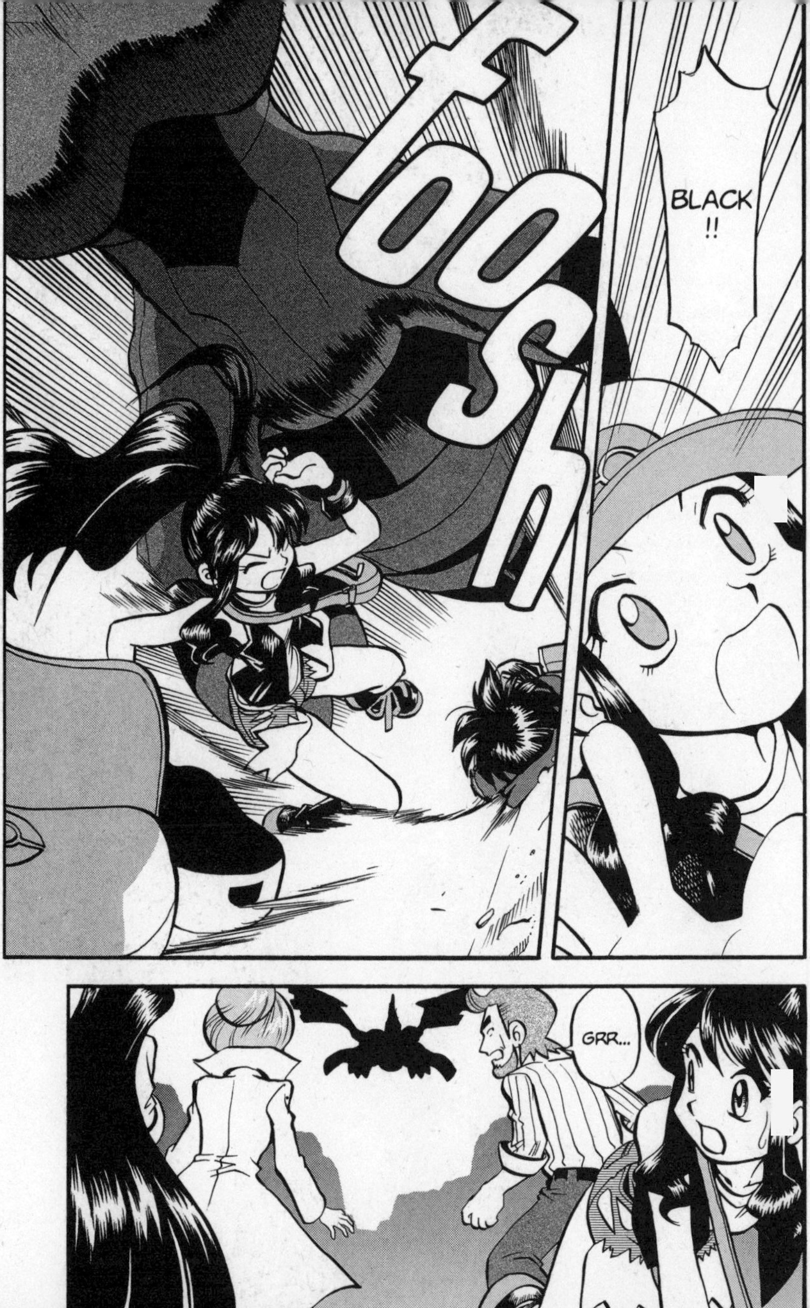
BLACK !!
fooSh
GRR...

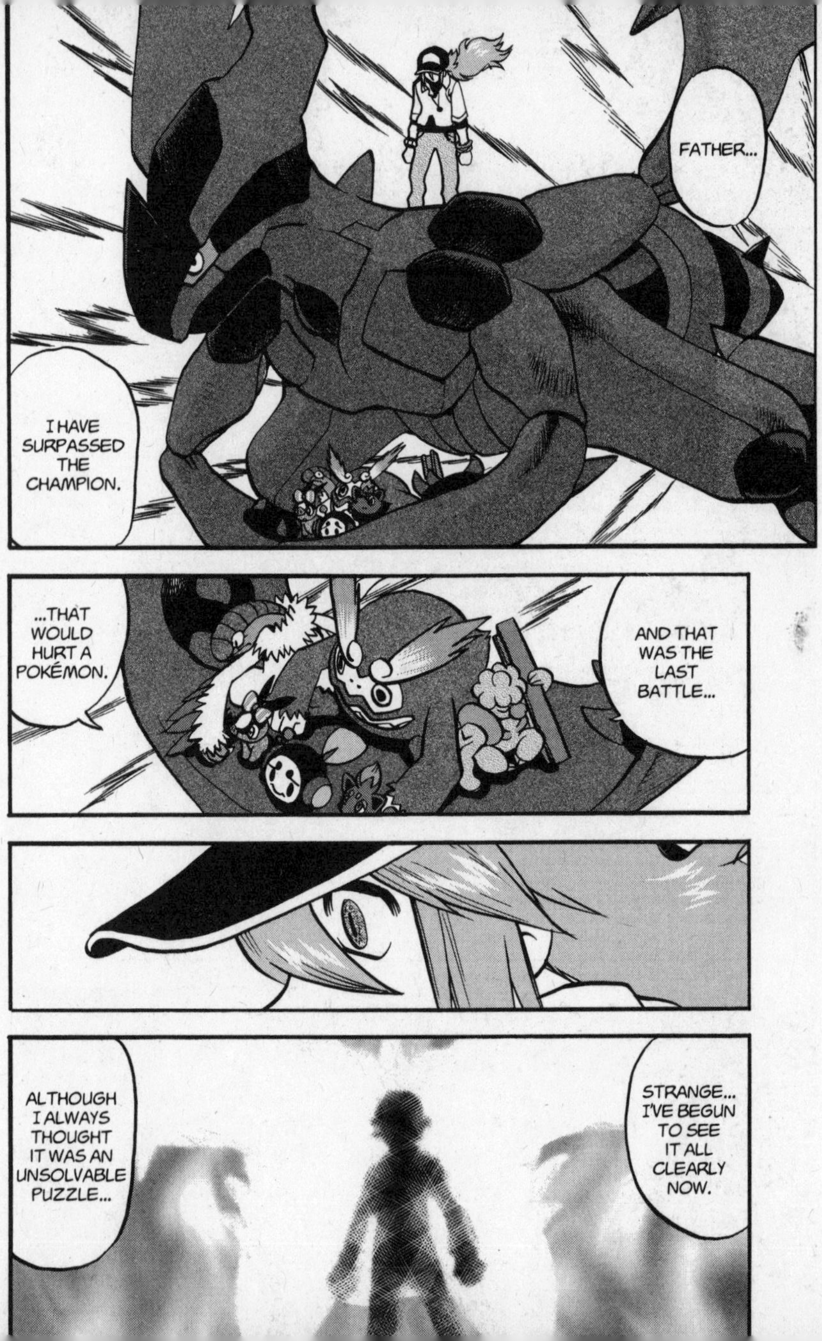
FATHER...
I HAVE SURPASSED THE CHAMPION.
AND THAT WAS THE LAST BATTLE...
...THAT WOULD HURT A POKÉMON.
STRANGE... I'VE BEGUN TO SEE IT ALL CLEARLY NOW.
ALTHOUGH I ALWAYS THOUGHT IT WAS AN UNSOLVABLE PUZZLE...

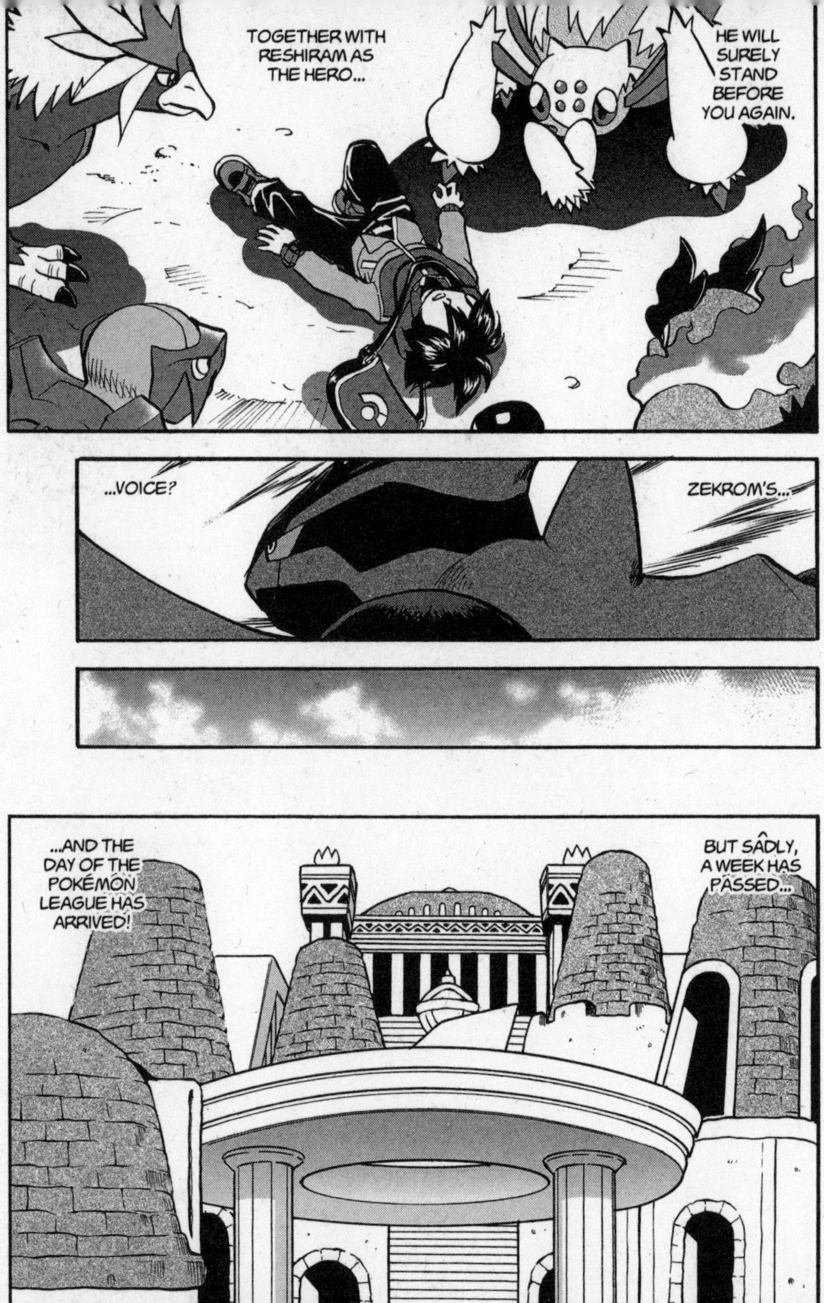
HE WILL SURELY STAND BEFORE YOU AGAIN.
TOGETHER WITH RESHIRAM AS THE HERO...
ZEKROM'S...
...VOICE?
BUT SADLY, A WEEK HAS PASSED...
...AND THE DAY OF THE POKÉMON LEAGUE HAS ARRIVED!

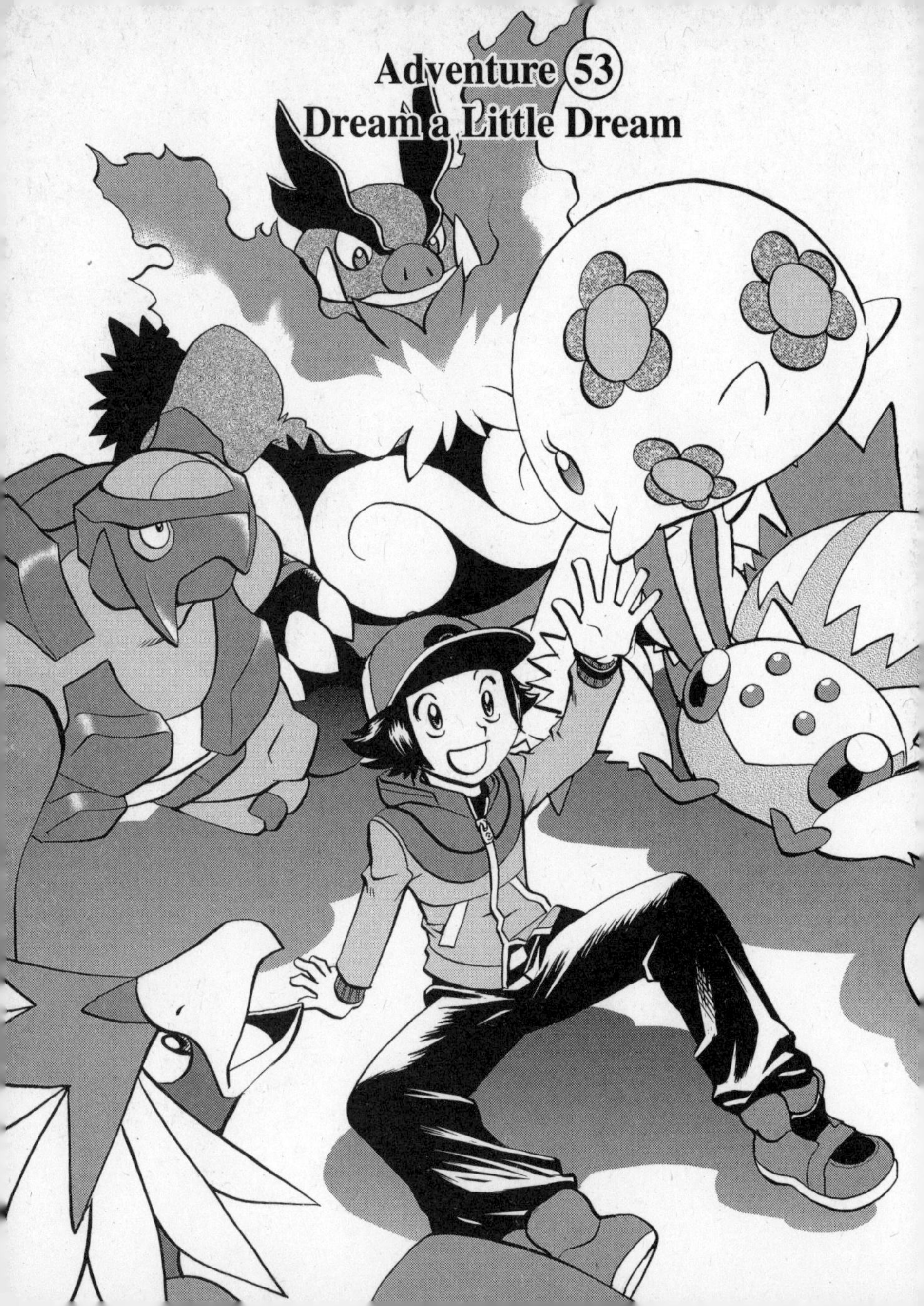
Adventure 53
Dream a Little Dream

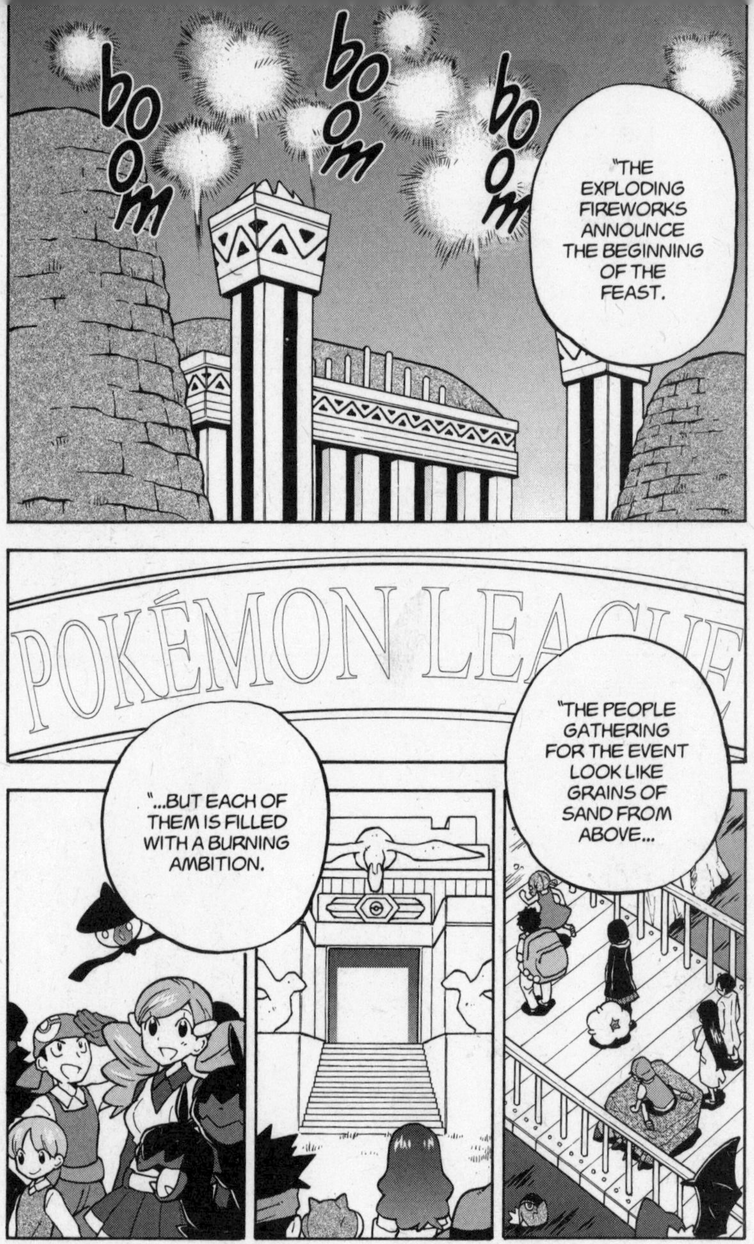

"THE EXPLODING FIREWORKS ANNOUNCE THE BEGINNING OF THE FEAST.
boom
boom
boom
POKÉMON LEAGUE
"THE PEOPLE GATHERING FOR THE EVENT LOOK LIKE GRAINS OF SAND FROM ABOVE...
"...BUT EACH OF THEM IS FILLED WITH A BURNING AMBITION.

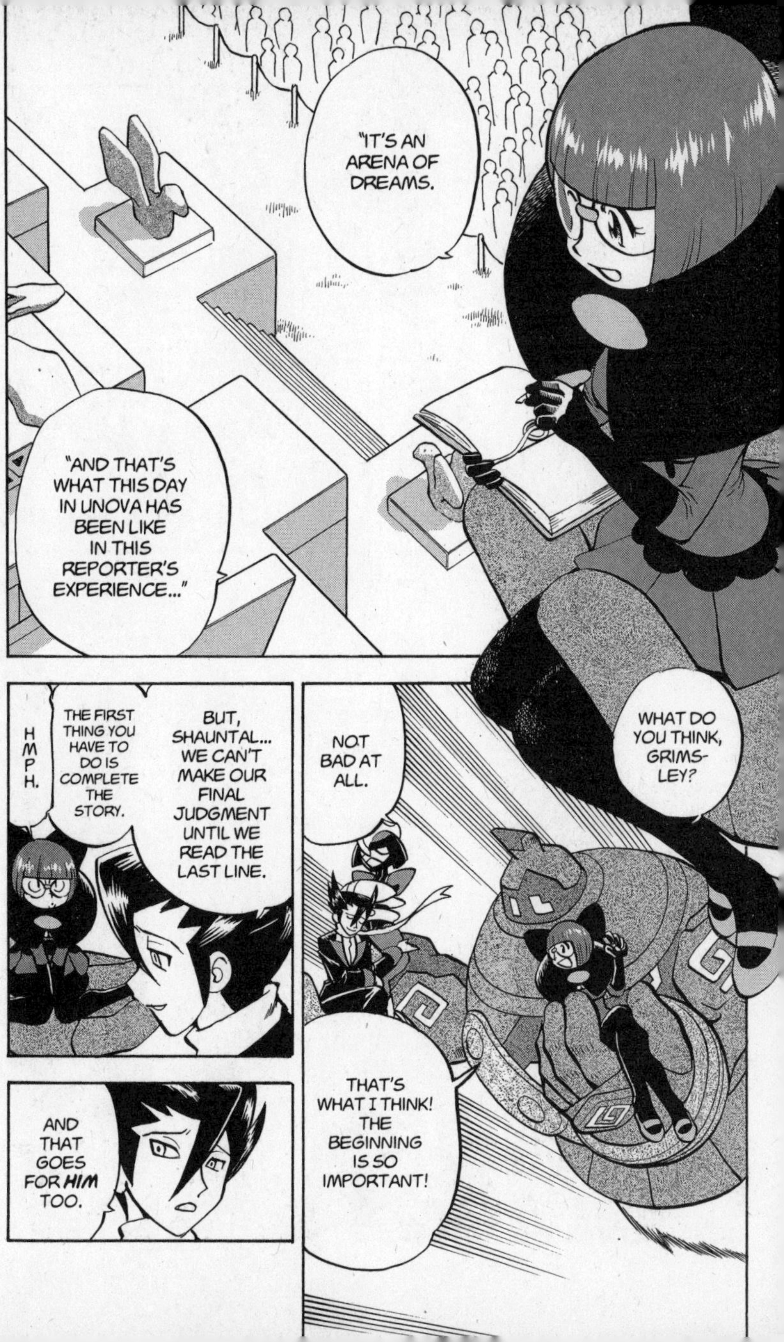
"IT'S AN ARENA OF DREAMS.
"AND THAT'S WHAT THIS DAY IN UNOVA HAS BEEN LIKE IN THIS REPORTER'S EXPERIENCE..."
WHAT DO YOU THINK, GRIMS-LEY?
NOT BAD AT ALL.
THAT'S WHAT I THINK! THE BEGINNING IS SO IMPORTANT!
BUT, SHAUNTAL... WE CAN'T MAKE OUR FINAL JUDGMENT UNTIL WE READ THE LAST LINE.
THE FIRST THING YOU HAVE TO DO IS COMPLETE THE STORY.
HMPH.
AND THAT GOES FOR **HIM** TOO.

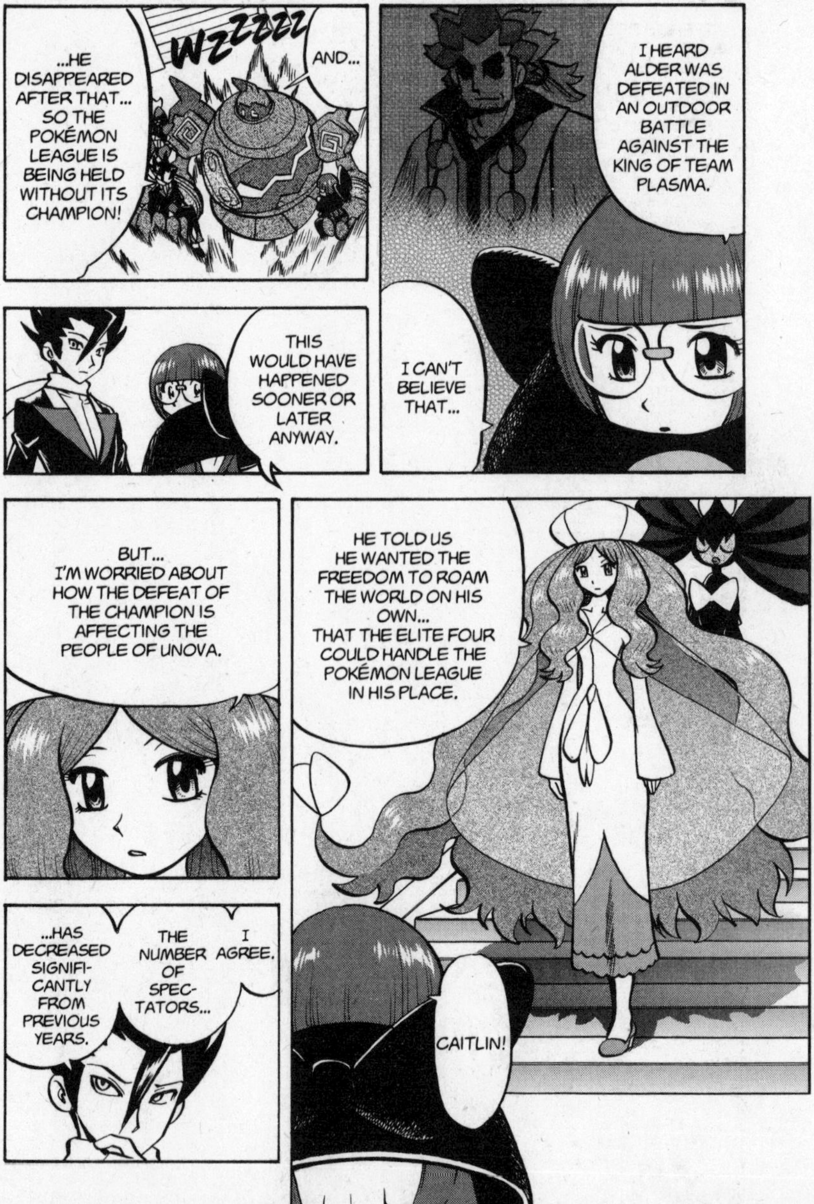
I HEARD ALDER WAS DEFEATED IN AN OUTDOOR BATTLE AGAINST THE KING OF TEAM PLASMA.
I CAN'T BELIEVE THAT...
AND...
WZZZZZ
...HE DISAPPEARED AFTER THAT... SO THE POKÉMON LEAGUE IS BEING HELD WITHOUT ITS CHAMPION!
THIS WOULD HAVE HAPPENED SOONER OR LATER ANYWAY.
HE TOLD US HE WANTED THE FREEDOM TO ROAM THE WORLD ON HIS OWN... THAT THE ELITE FOUR COULD HANDLE THE POKÉMON LEAGUE IN HIS PLACE.
CAITLIN!
BUT... I'M WORRIED ABOUT HOW THE DEFEAT OF THE CHAMPION IS AFFECTING THE PEOPLE OF UNOVA.
I AGREE.
THE NUMBER OF SPEC-TATORS...
...HAS DECREASED SIGNIFI-CANTLY FROM PREVIOUS YEARS.

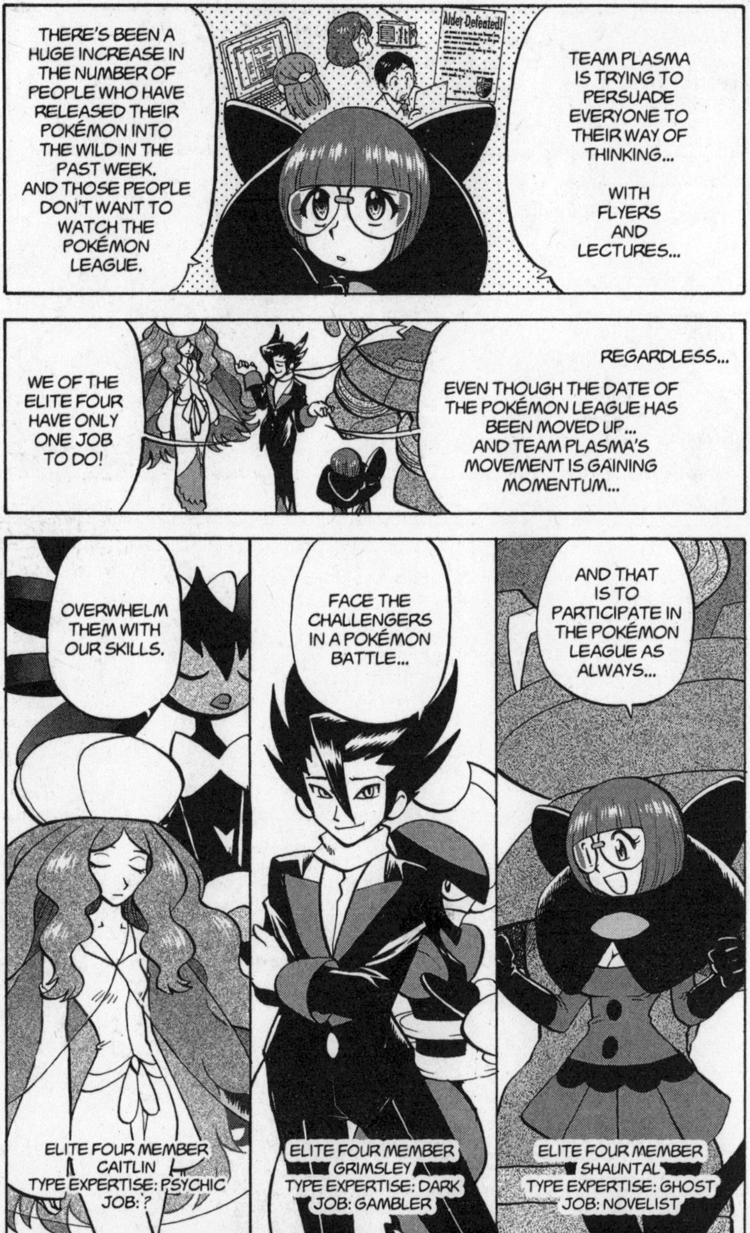
TEAM PLASMA IS TRYING TO PERSUADE EVERYONE TO THEIR WAY OF THINKING...
WITH FLYERS AND LECTURES...
Alder Defeated!
THERE'S BEEN A HUGE INCREASE IN THE NUMBER OF PEOPLE WHO HAVE RELEASED THEIR POKÉMON INTO THE WILD IN THE PAST WEEK. AND THOSE PEOPLE DON'T WANT TO WATCH THE POKÉMON LEAGUE.
REGARDLESS...
EVEN THOUGH THE DATE OF THE POKÉMON LEAGUE HAS BEEN MOVED UP... AND TEAM PLASMA'S MOVEMENT IS GAINING MOMENTUM...
WE OF THE ELITE FOUR HAVE ONLY ONE JOB TO DO!
AND THAT IS TO PARTICIPATE IN THE POKÉMON LEAGUE AS ALWAYS...
ELITE FOUR MEMBER SHAUNTAL TYPE EXPERTISE: GHOST JOB: NOVELIST
FACE THE CHALLENGERS IN A POKÉMON BATTLE...
ELITE FOUR MEMBER GRIMSLEY TYPE EXPERTISE: DARK JOB: GAMBLER
OVERWHELM THEM WITH OUR SKILLS.
ELITE FOUR MEMBER CAITLIN TYPE EXPERTISE: PSYCHIC JOB: ?

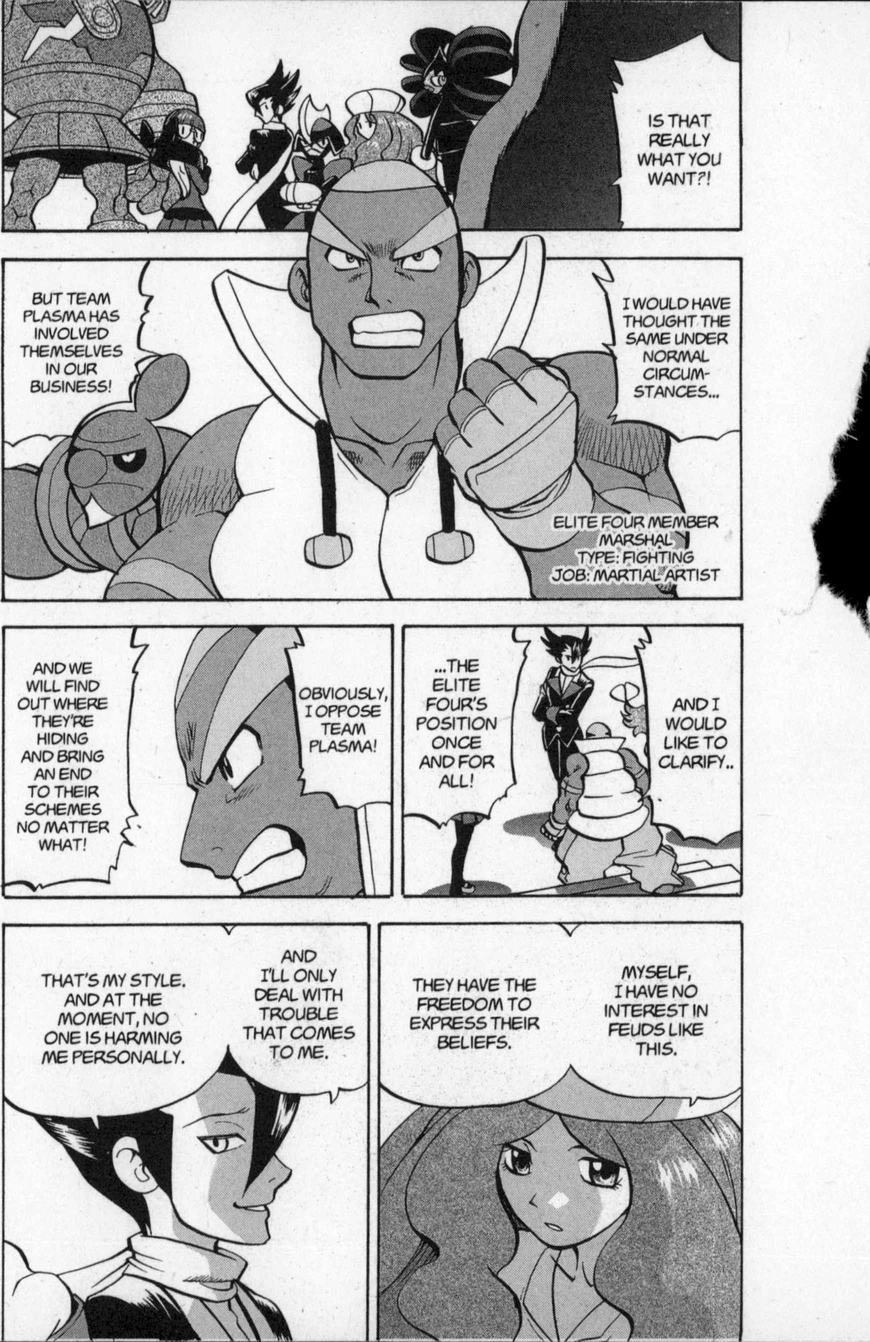
IS THAT REALLY WHAT YOU WANT?!
I WOULD HAVE THOUGHT THE SAME UNDER NORMAL CIRCUM-STANCES...
BUT TEAM PLASMA HAS INVOLVED THEMSELVES IN OUR BUSINESS!
ELITE FOUR MEMBER MARSHAL TYPE: FIGHTING JOB: MARTIAL ARTIST
AND I WOULD LIKE TO CLARIFY..
...THE ELITE FOUR'S POSITION ONCE AND FOR ALL!
OBVIOUSLY, I OPPOSE TEAM PLASMA!
AND WE WILL FIND OUT WHERE THEY'RE HIDING AND BRING AN END TO THEIR SCHEMES NO MATTER WHAT!
MYSELF, I HAVE NO INTEREST IN FEUDS LIKE THIS.
THEY HAVE THE FREEDOM TO EXPRESS THEIR BELIEFS.
AND I'LL ONLY DEAL WITH TROUBLE THAT COMES TO ME.
THAT'S MY STYLE. AND AT THE MOMENT, NO ONE IS HARMING ME PERSONALLY.

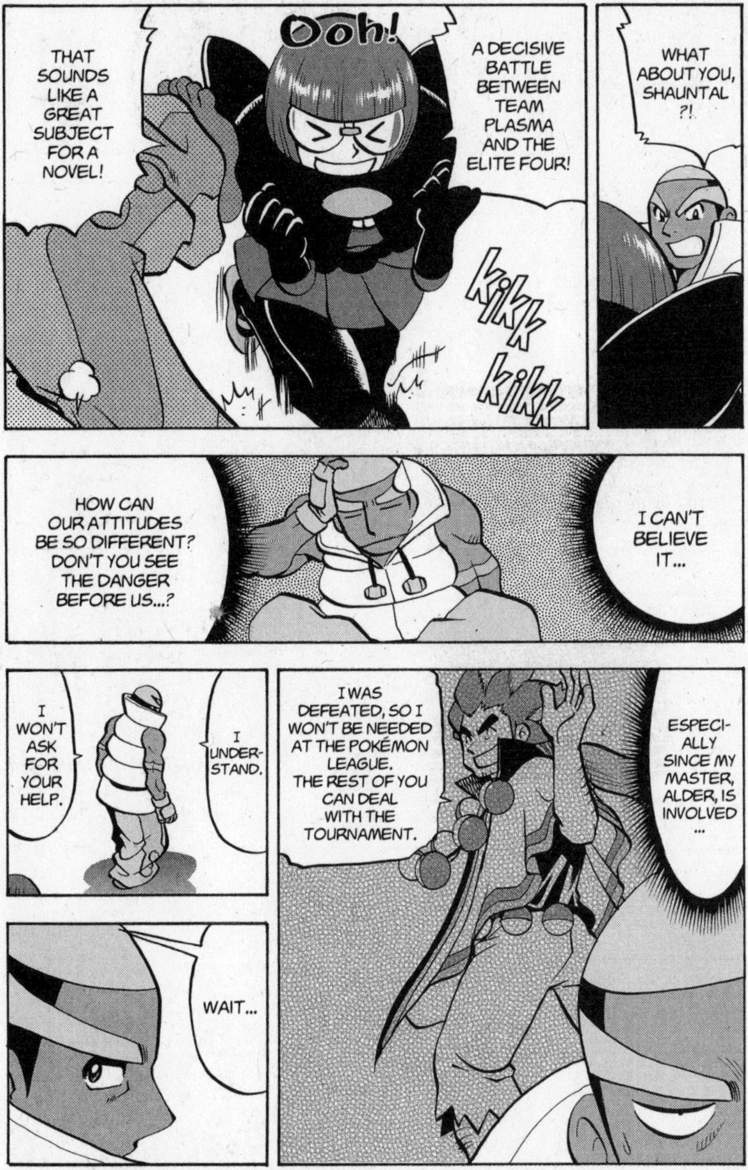
WHAT ABOUT YOU, SHAUNTAL?!
Ooh!
A DECISIVE BATTLE BETWEEN TEAM PLASMA AND THE ELITE FOUR!
THAT SOUNDS LIKE A GREAT SUBJECT FOR A NOVEL!
kikk kikk
I CAN'T BELIEVE IT...
HOW CAN OUR ATTITUDES BE SO DIFFERENT? DON'T YOU SEE THE DANGER BEFORE US...?
ESPECIALLY SINCE MY MASTER, ALDER, IS INVOLVED...
I WAS DEFEATED, SO I WON'T BE NEEDED AT THE POKÉMON LEAGUE. THE REST OF YOU CAN DEAL WITH THE TOURNAMENT.
I UNDERSTAND.
I WON'T ASK FOR YOUR HELP.
WAIT...

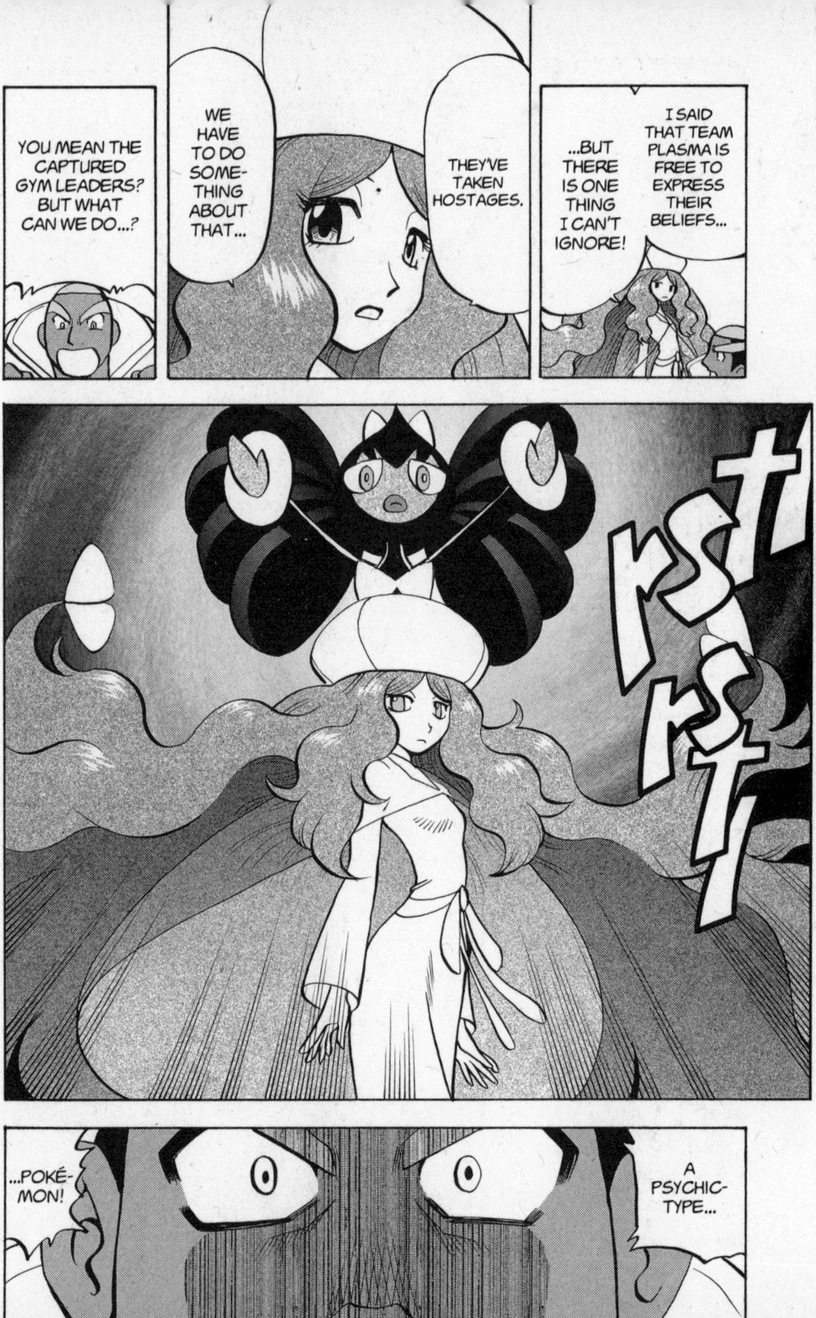
I SAID THAT TEAM PLASMA IS FREE TO EXPRESS THEIR BELIEFS...
...BUT THERE IS ONE THING I CAN'T IGNORE!
THEY'VE TAKEN HOSTAGES.
WE HAVE TO DO SOME-THING ABOUT THAT...
YOU MEAN THE CAPTURED GYM LEADERS? BUT WHAT CAN WE DO...?
A PSYCHIC-TYPE...
...POKÉ-MON!

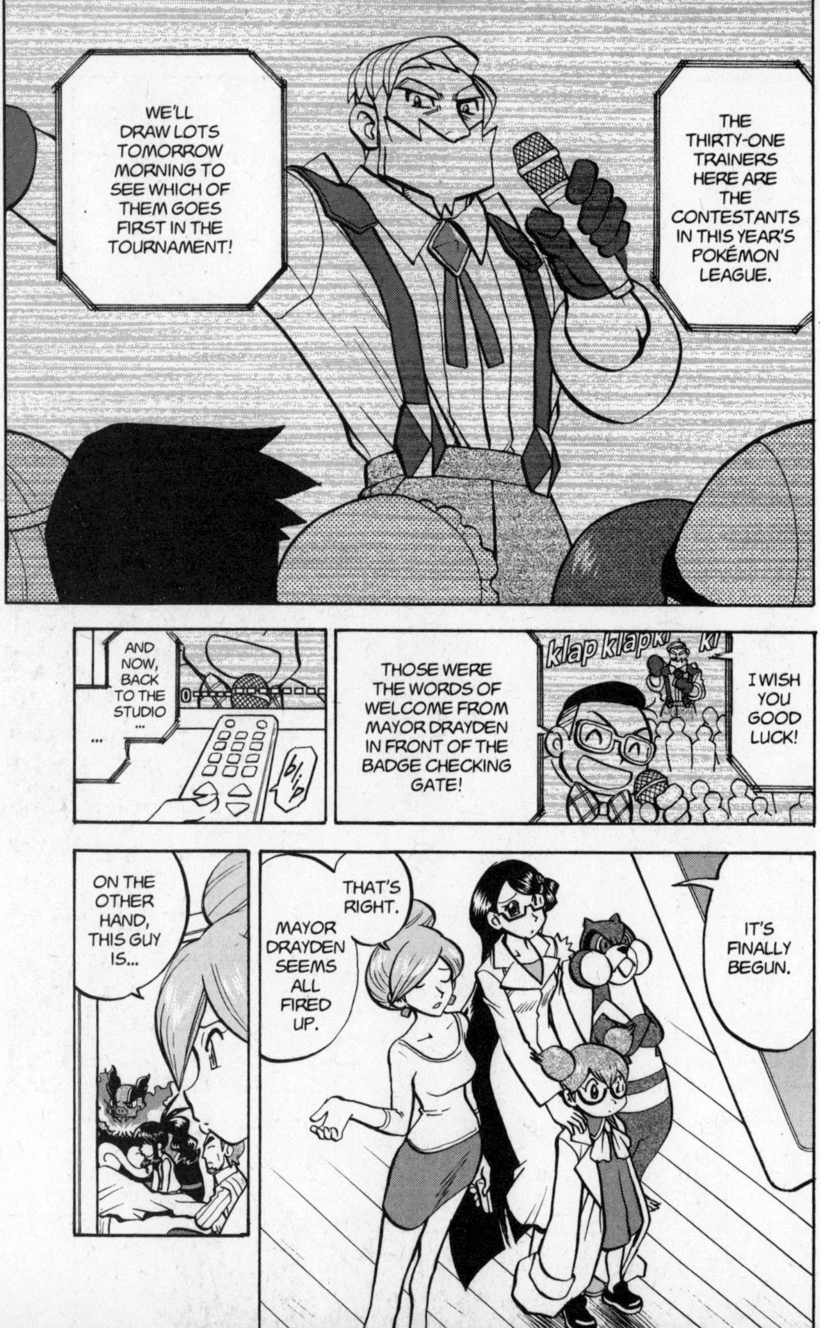

THE THIRTY-ONE TRAINERS HERE ARE THE CONTESTANTS IN THIS YEAR'S POKÉMON LEAGUE.
WE'LL DRAW LOTS TOMORROW MORNING TO SEE WHICH OF THEM GOES FIRST IN THE TOURNAMENT!
klap klapkl kl
I WISH YOU GOOD LUCK!
THOSE WERE THE WORDS OF WELCOME FROM MAYOR DRAYDEN IN FRONT OF THE BADGE CHECKING GATE!
AND NOW, BACK TO THE STUDIO ...
...
blip
IT'S FINALLY BEGUN.
THAT'S RIGHT.
MAYOR DRAYDEN SEEMS ALL FIRED UP.
ON THE OTHER HAND, THIS GUY IS...

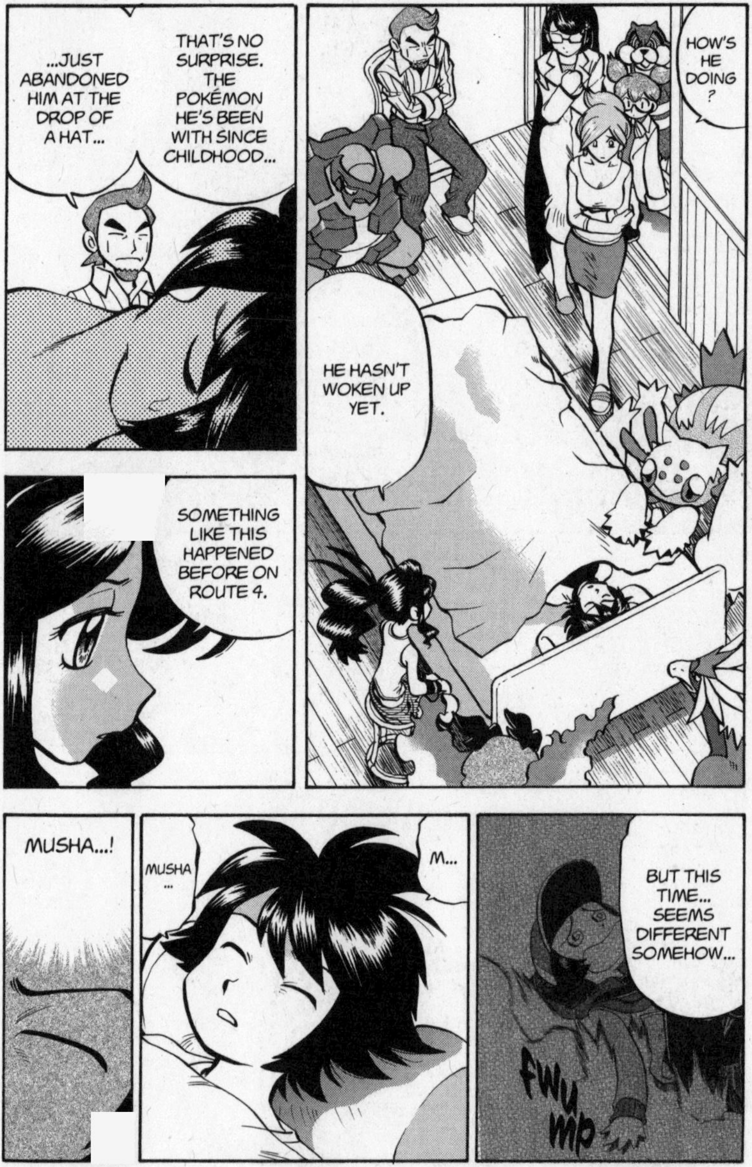
HOW'S HE DOING?
HE HASN'T WOKEN UP YET.
THAT'S NO SURPRISE. THE POKÉMON HE'S BEEN WITH SINCE CHILDHOOD...
...JUST ABANDONED HIM AT THE DROP OF A HAT...
SOMETHING LIKE THIS HAPPENED BEFORE ON ROUTE 4.
BUT THIS TIME... SEEMS DIFFERENT SOMEHOW...
fwuump
M...
MUSHA...
MUSHA...!

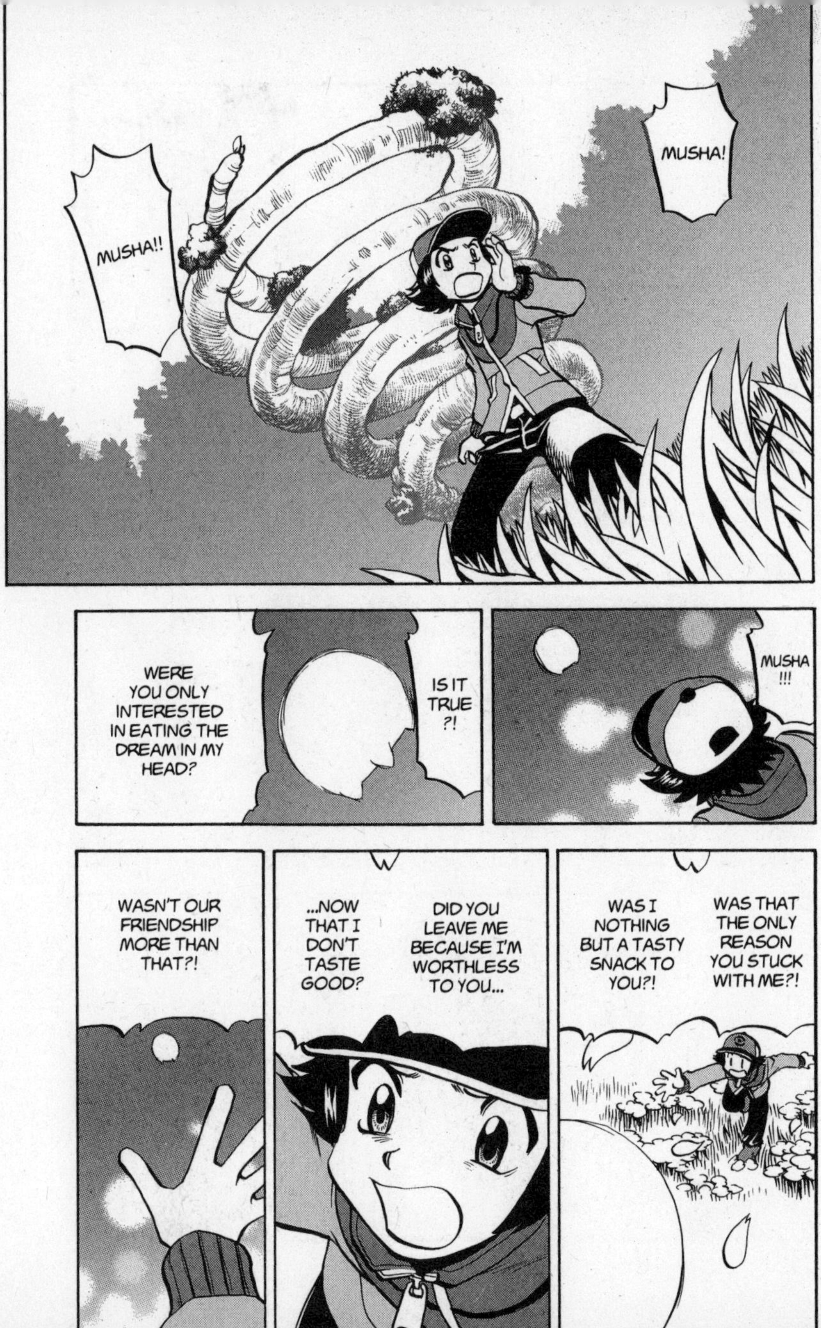
MUSHA!
MUSHA!!
MUSHA !!!
IS IT TRUE ?!
WERE YOU ONLY INTERESTED IN EATING THE DREAM IN MY HEAD?
WAS THAT THE ONLY REASON YOU STUCK WITH ME?!
WAS I NOTHING BUT A TASTY SNACK TO YOU?!
DID YOU LEAVE ME BECAUSE I'M WORTHLESS TO YOU...
...NOW THAT I DON'T TASTE GOOD?
WASN'T OUR FRIENDSHIP MORE THAN THAT?!

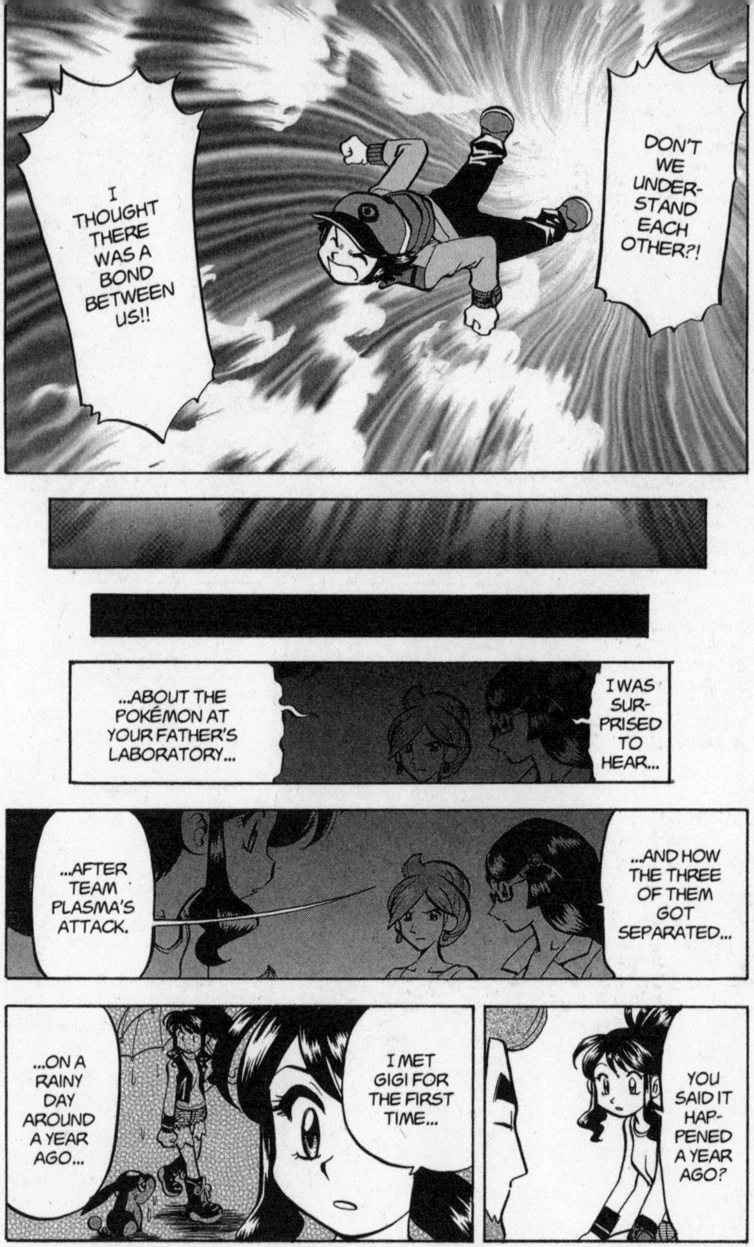
DON'T WE UNDER-STAND EACH OTHER?!
I THOUGHT THERE WAS A BOND BETWEEN US!!
I WAS SUR-PRISED TO HEAR...
...ABOUT THE POKÉMON AT YOUR FATHER'S LABORATORY...
...AND HOW THE THREE OF THEM GOT SEPARATED...
...AFTER TEAM PLASMA'S ATTACK.
YOU SAID IT HAP-PENED A YEAR AGO?
I MET GIGI FOR THE FIRST TIME...
...ON A RAINY DAY AROUND A YEAR AGO...

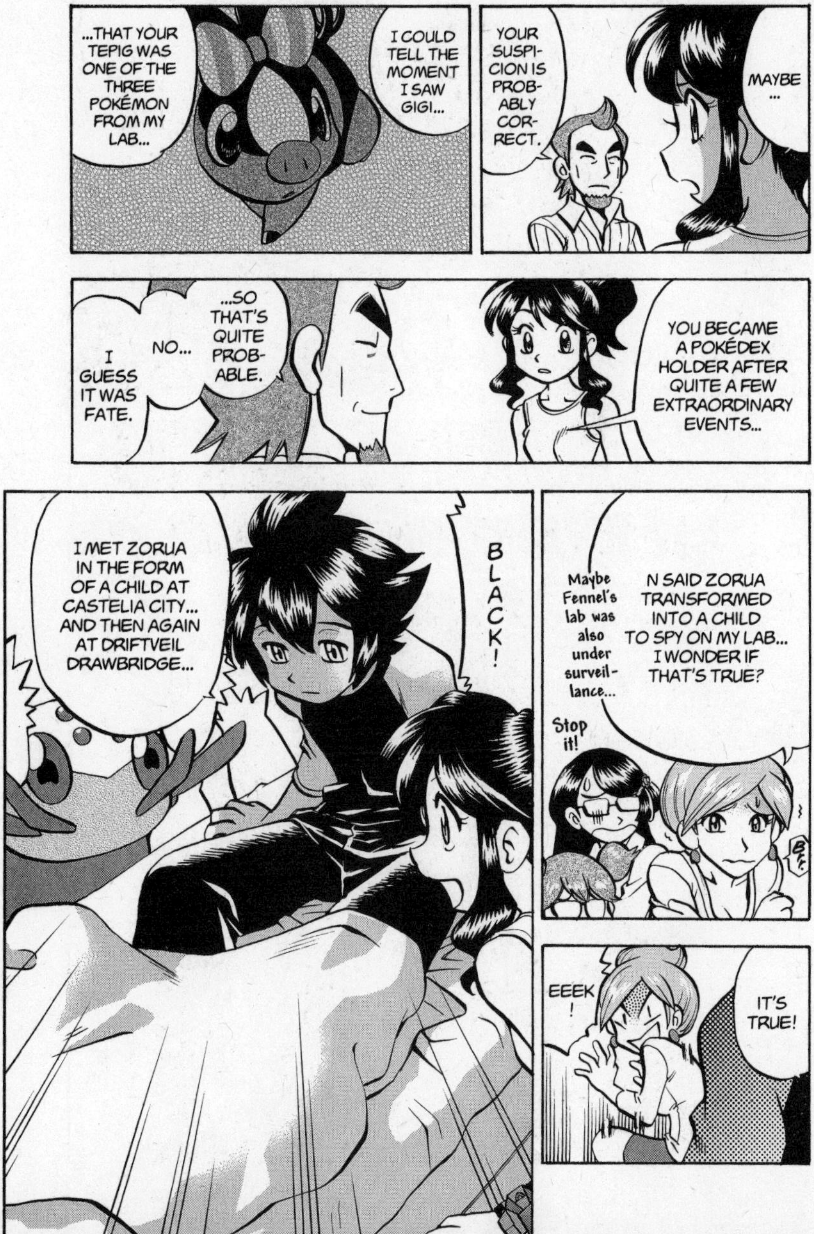
MAYBE...
YOUR SUSPICION IS PROBABLY CORRECT.
I COULD TELL THE MOMENT I SAW GIGI...
...THAT YOUR TEPIG WAS ONE OF THE THREE POKÉMON FROM MY LAB...
YOU BECAME A POKÉDEX HOLDER AFTER QUITE A FEW EXTRAORDINARY EVENTS...
...SO THAT'S QUITE PROBABLE.
NO...
I GUESS IT WAS FATE.
N SAID ZORUA TRANSFORMED INTO A CHILD TO SPY ON MY LAB... I WONDER IF THAT'S TRUE?
Maybe Fennel's lab was also under surveillance...
Stop it!
IT'S TRUE!
EEEK!
BLACK!
I MET ZORUA IN THE FORM OF A CHILD AT CASTELIA CITY... AND THEN AGAIN AT DRIFTVEIL DRAWBRIDGE...

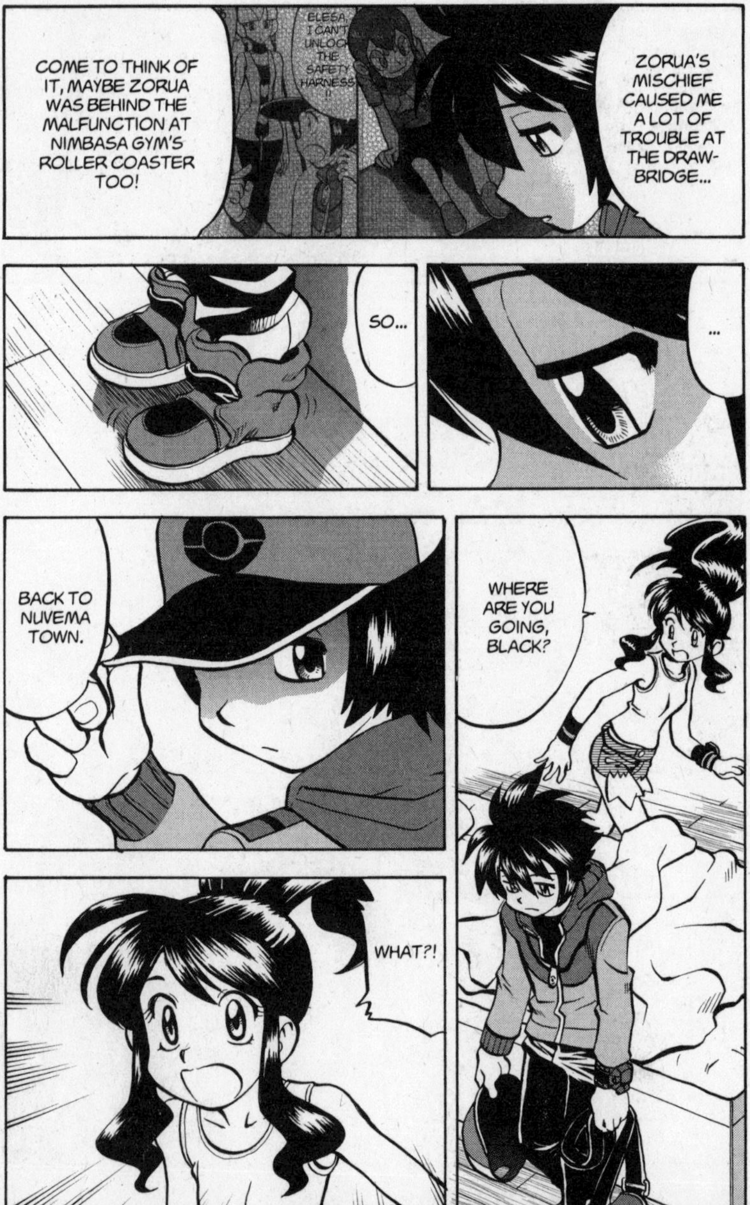

ZORUA'S MISCHIEF CAUSED ME A LOT OF TROUBLE AT THE DRAW-BRIDGE...
ELESA, I CAN'T UNLOC THE SAFETY HARNESS!!
COME TO THINK OF IT, MAYBE ZORUA WAS BEHIND THE MALFUNCTION AT NIMBASA GYM'S ROLLER COASTER TOO!
...
SO...
WHERE ARE YOU GOING, BLACK?
BACK TO NUVEMA TOWN.
WHAT?!

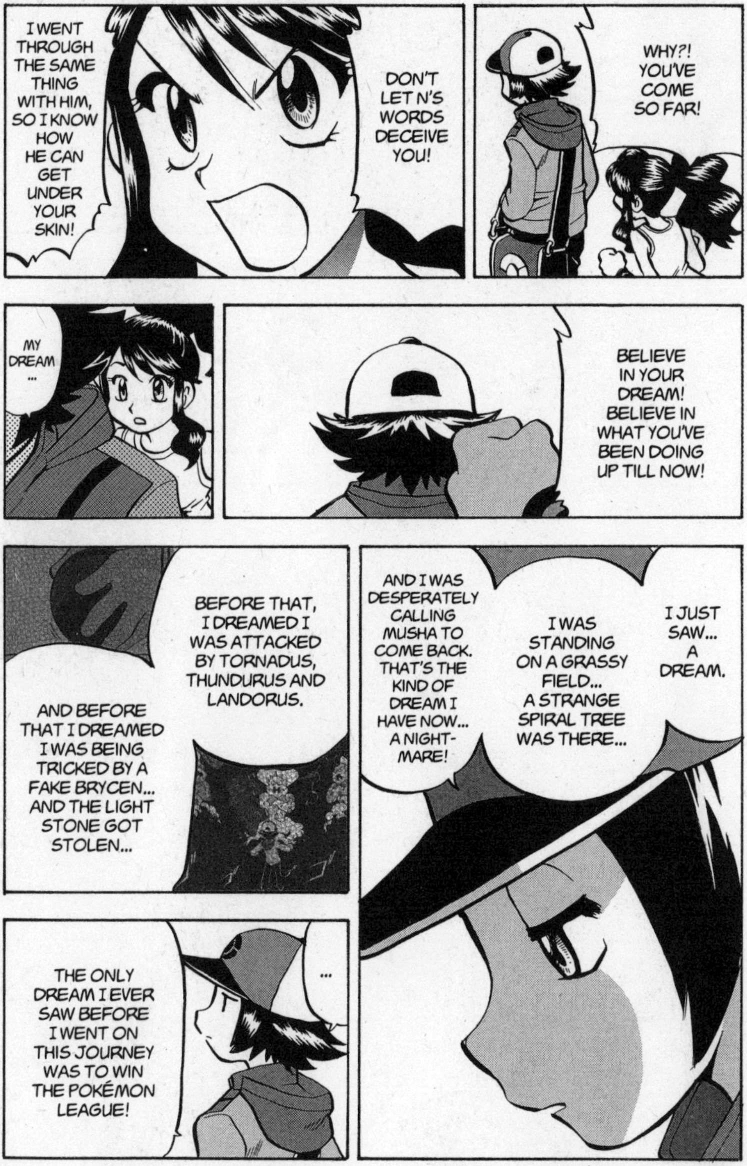
WHY?! YOU'VE COME SO FAR!
DON'T LET N'S WORDS DECEIVE YOU!
I WENT THROUGH THE SAME THING WITH HIM, SO I KNOW HOW HE CAN GET UNDER YOUR SKIN!
BELIEVE IN YOUR DREAM! BELIEVE IN WHAT YOU'VE BEEN DOING UP TILL NOW!
MY DREAM...
I JUST SAW... A DREAM.
I WAS STANDING ON A GRASSY FIELD... A STRANGE SPIRAL TREE WAS THERE...
AND I WAS DESPERATELY CALLING MUSHA TO COME BACK. THAT'S THE KIND OF DREAM I HAVE NOW... A NIGHT-MARE!
BEFORE THAT, I DREAMED I WAS ATTACKED BY TORNADUS, THUNDURUS AND LANDORUS.
AND BEFORE THAT I DREAMED I WAS BEING TRICKED BY A FAKE BRYCEN... AND THE LIGHT STONE GOT STOLEN...
...
THE ONLY DREAM I EVER SAW BEFORE I WENT ON THIS JOURNEY WAS TO WIN THE POKÉMON LEAGUE!

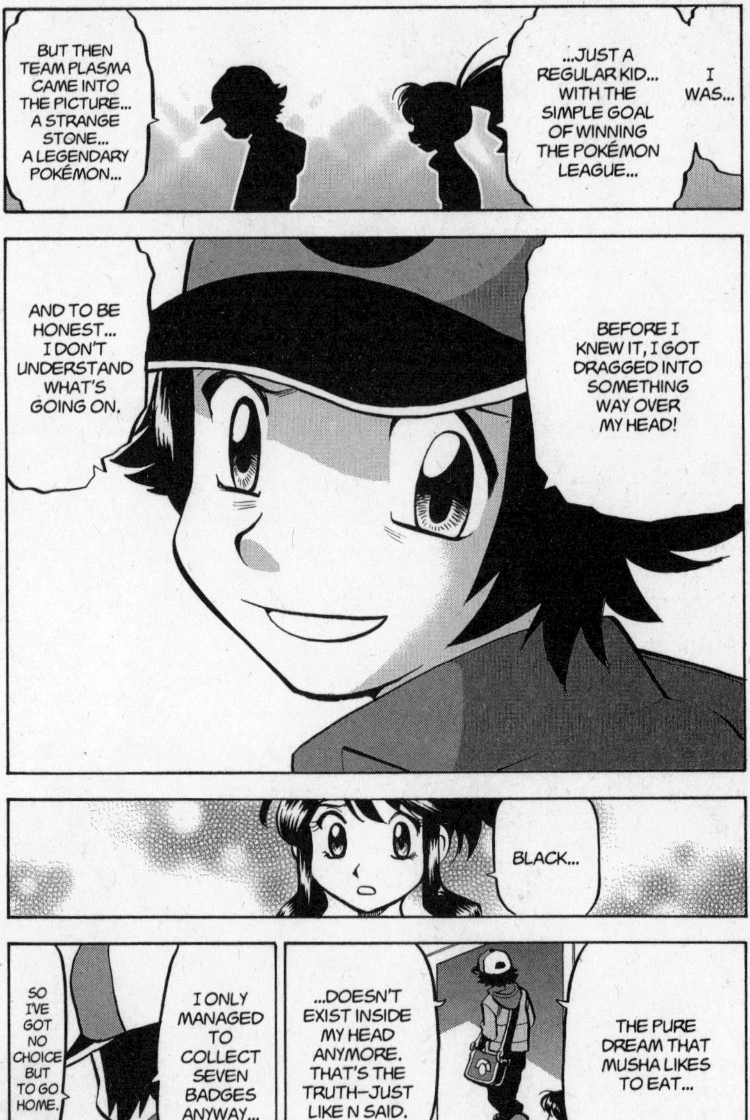
I WAS...
...JUST A REGULAR KID... WITH THE SIMPLE GOAL OF WINNING THE POKÉMON LEAGUE...
BUT THEN TEAM PLASMA CAME INTO THE PICTURE... A STRANGE STONE... A LEGENDARY POKÉMON...
BEFORE I KNEW IT, I GOT DRAGGED INTO SOMETHING WAY OVER MY HEAD!
AND TO BE HONEST... I DON'T UNDERSTAND WHAT'S GOING ON.
BLACK...
THE PURE DREAM THAT MUSHA LIKES TO EAT...
...DOESN'T EXIST INSIDE MY HEAD ANYMORE. THAT'S THE TRUTH—JUST LIKE N SAID.
I ONLY MANAGED TO COLLECT SEVEN BADGES ANYWAY...
SO I'VE GOT NO CHOICE BUT TO GO HOME.

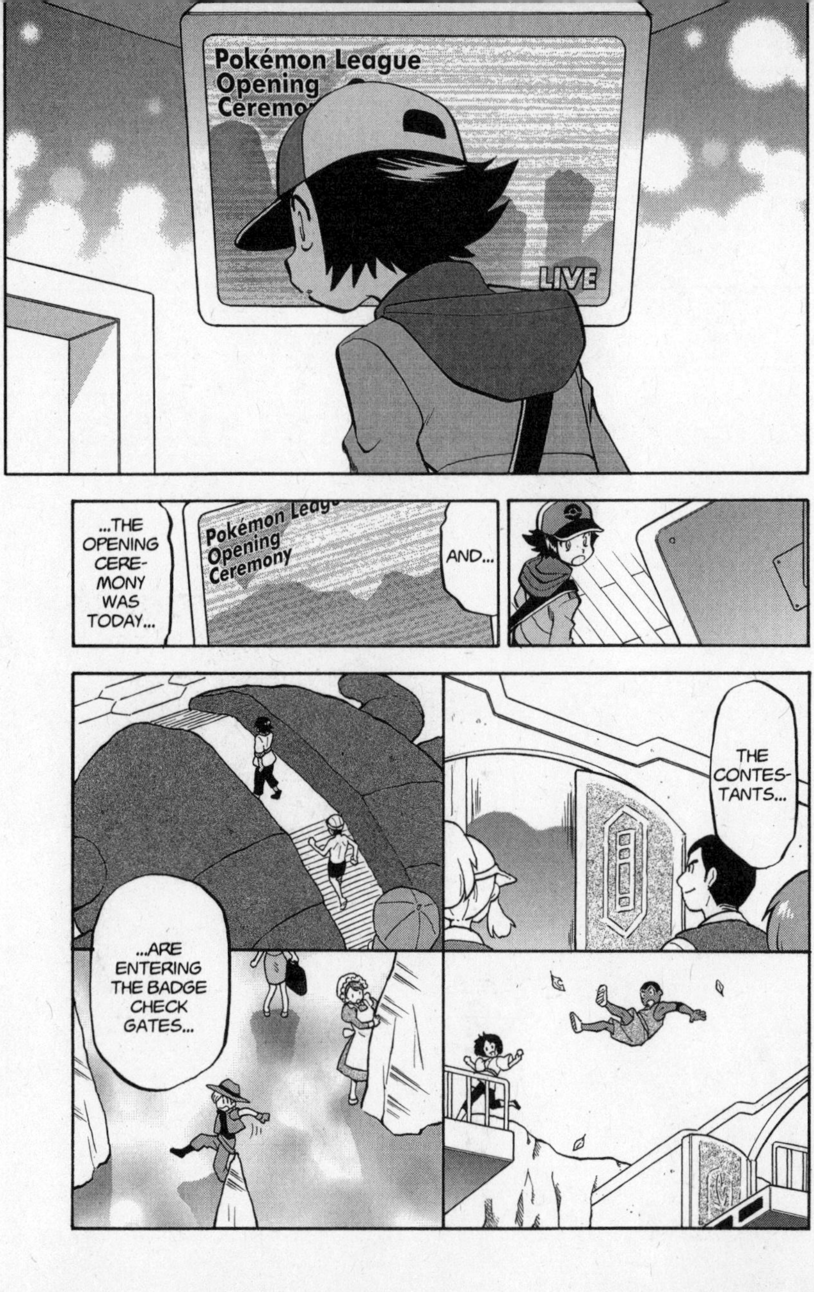

Pokémon League Opening Ceremo
LIVE
...THE OPENING CEREMONY WAS TODAY...
Pokémon Leag
Opening Ceremony
AND...
THE CONTESTANTS...
...ARE ENTERING THE BADGE CHECK GATES...

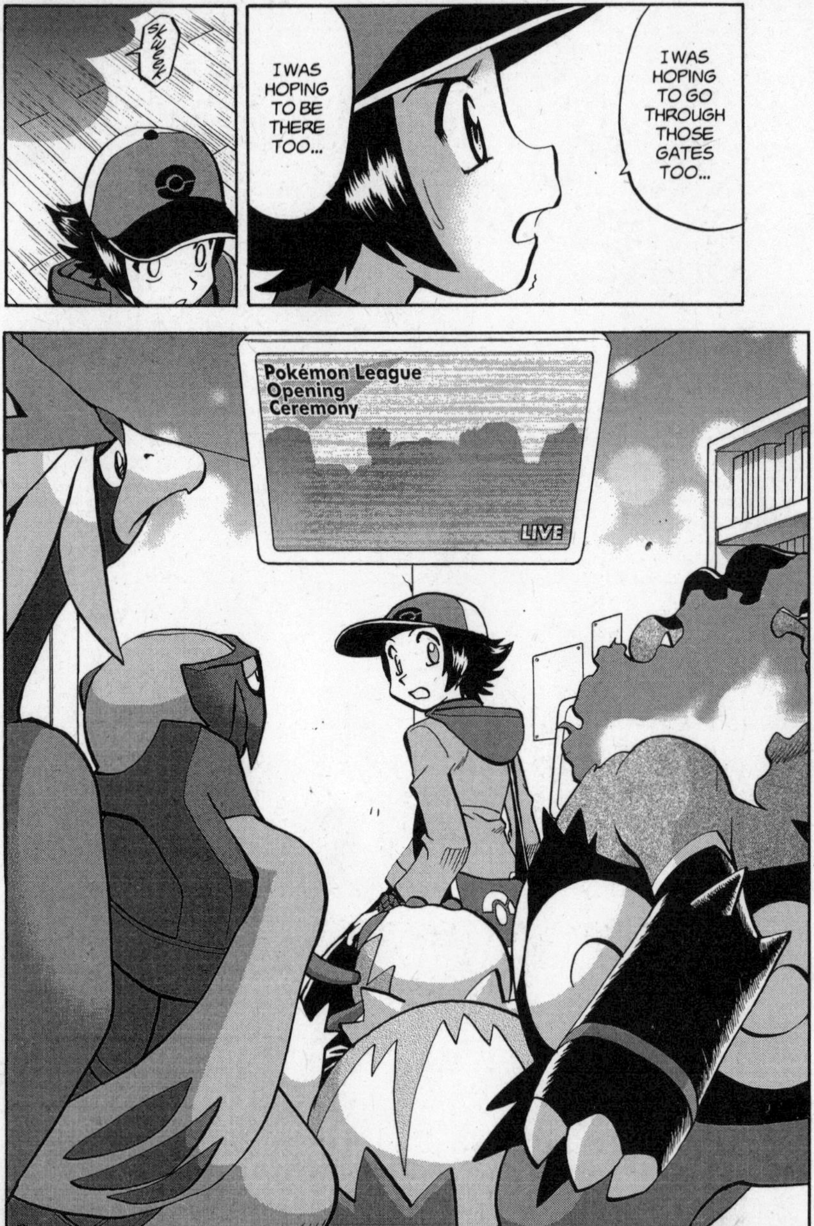
I WAS HOPING TO GO THROUGH THOSE GATES TOO...
I WAS HOPING TO BE THERE TOO...
SKWEEK
Pokémon League Opening Ceremony
LIVE

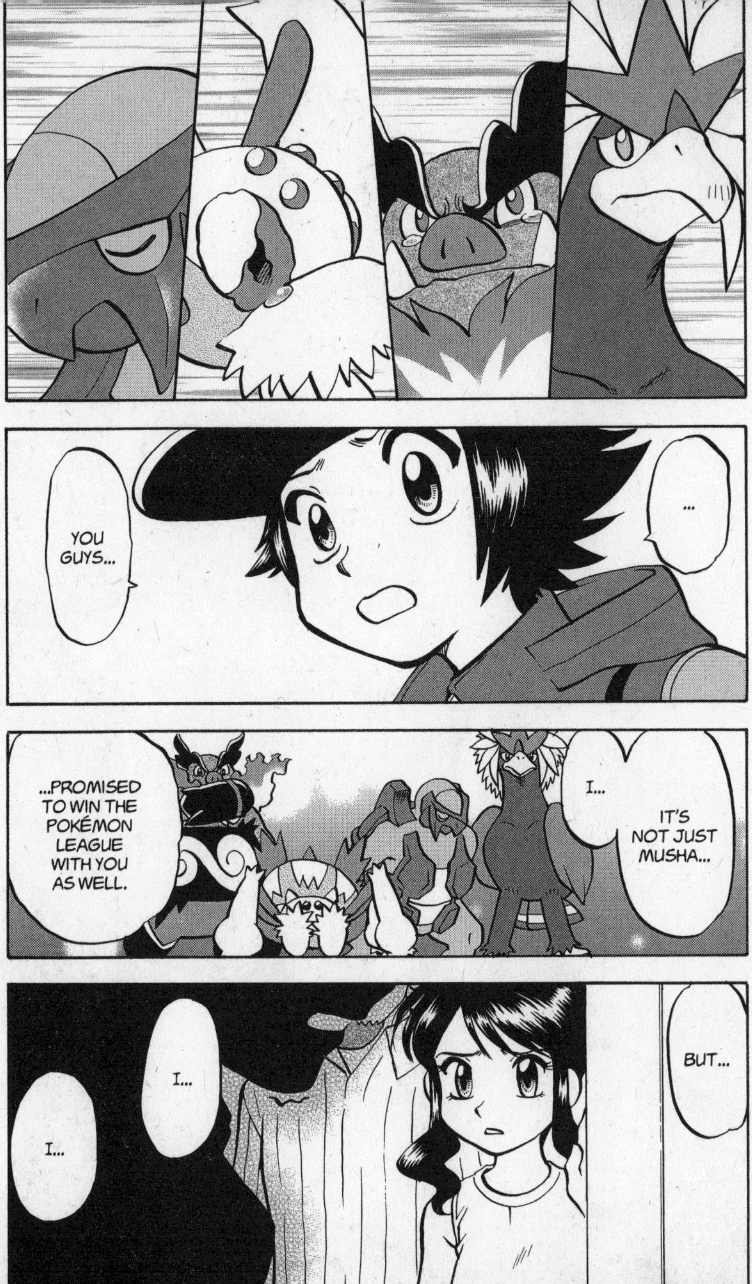
...
YOU GUYS...
I...
IT'S NOT JUST MUSHA...
...PROMISED TO WIN THE POKÉMON LEAGUE WITH YOU AS WELL.
BUT...
I...
I...

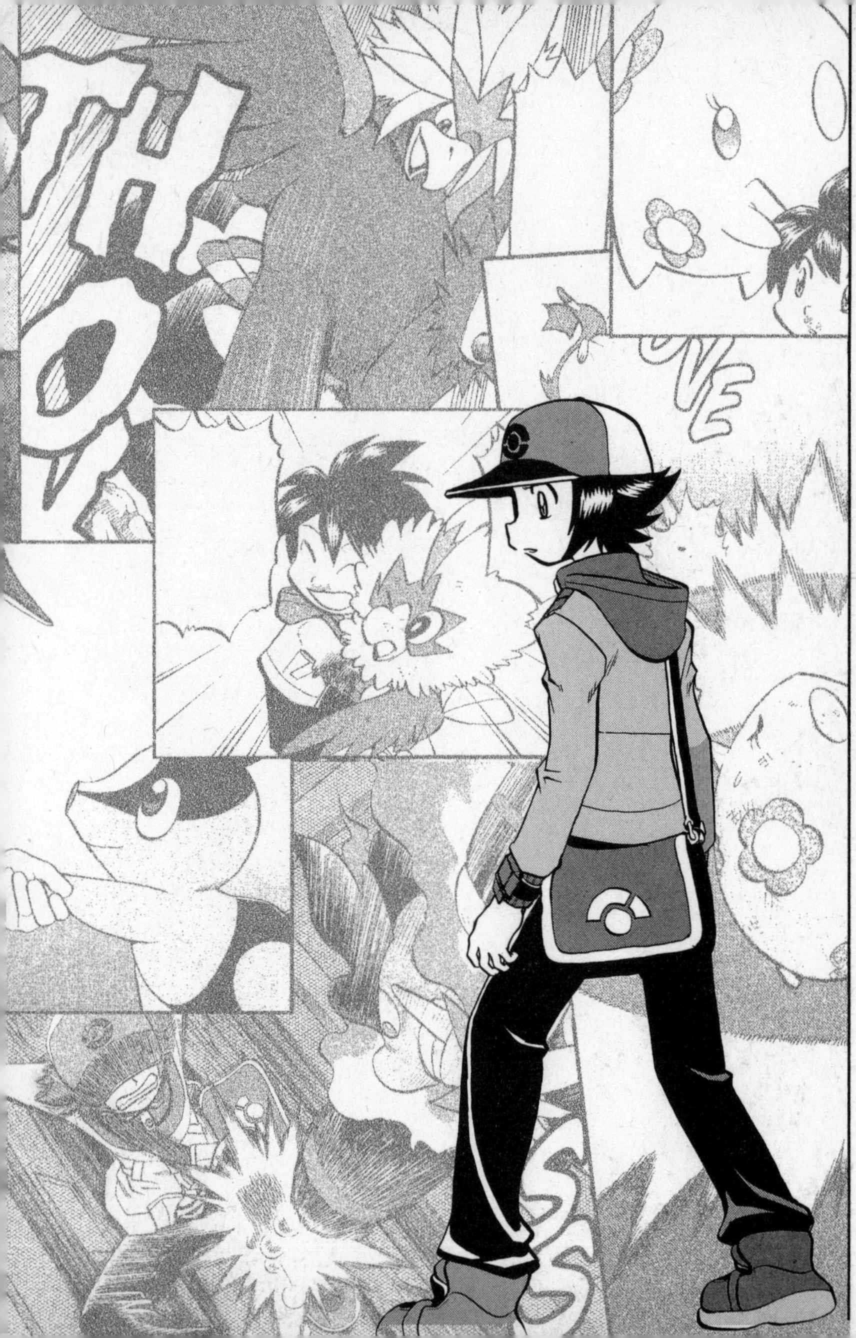

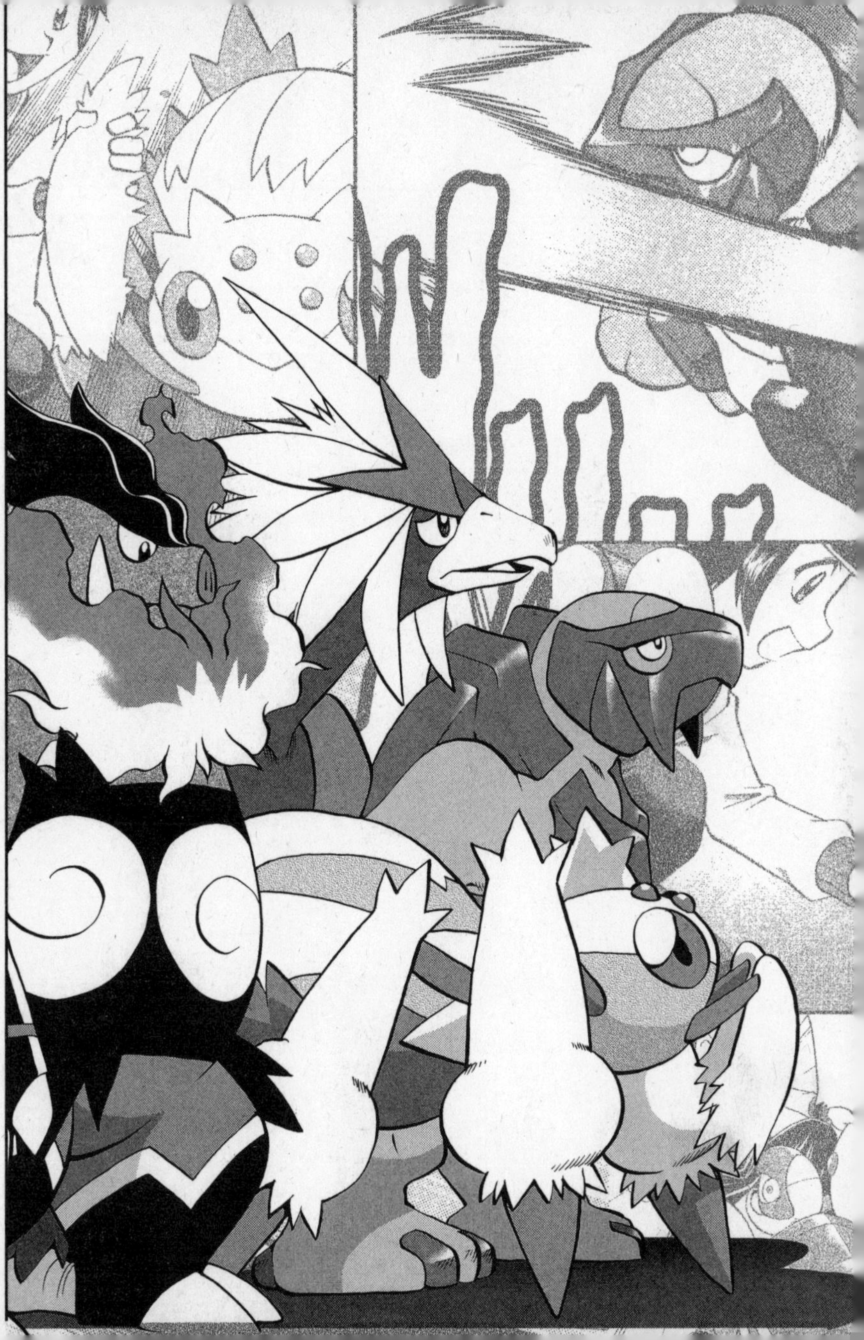

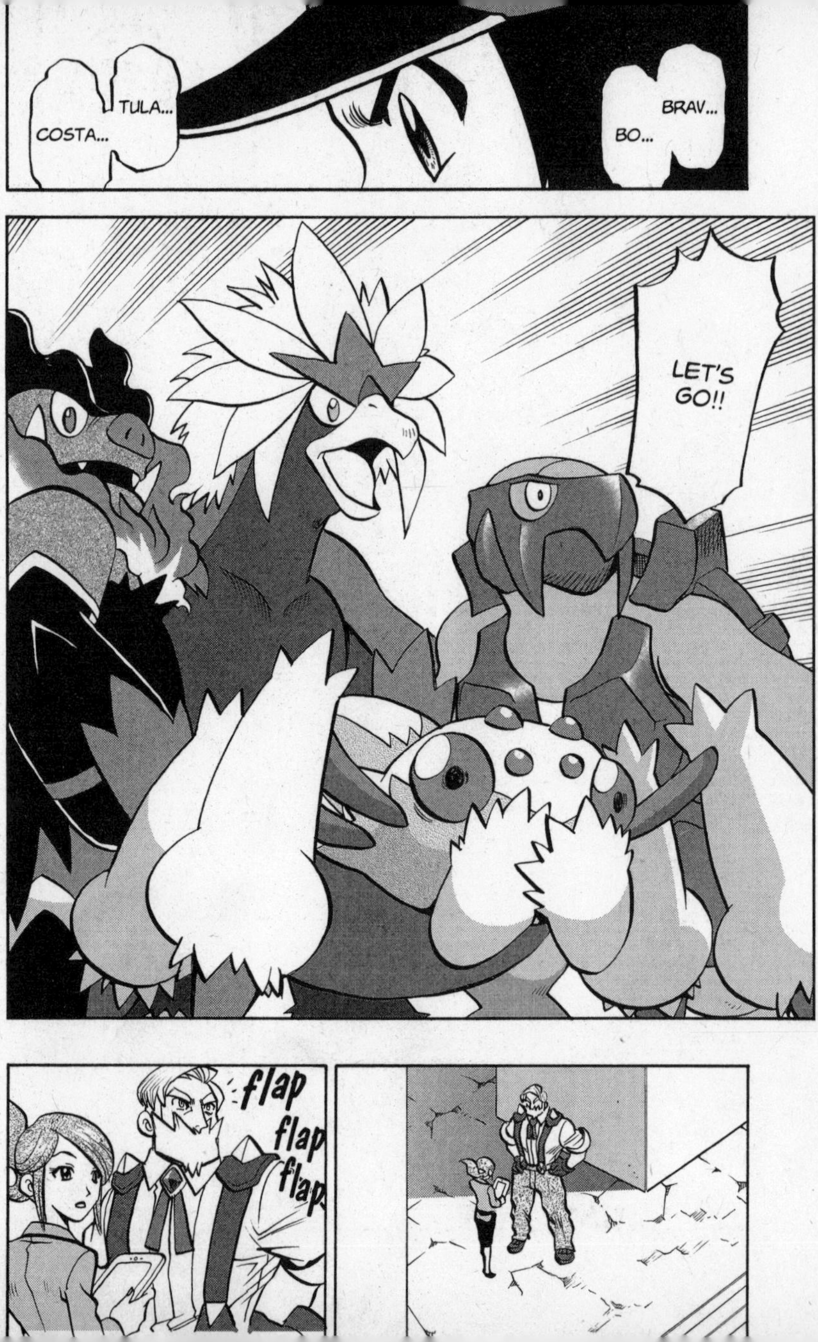
BRAV...
BO...
TULA...
COSTA...
LET'S GO!!
flap
flap
flap

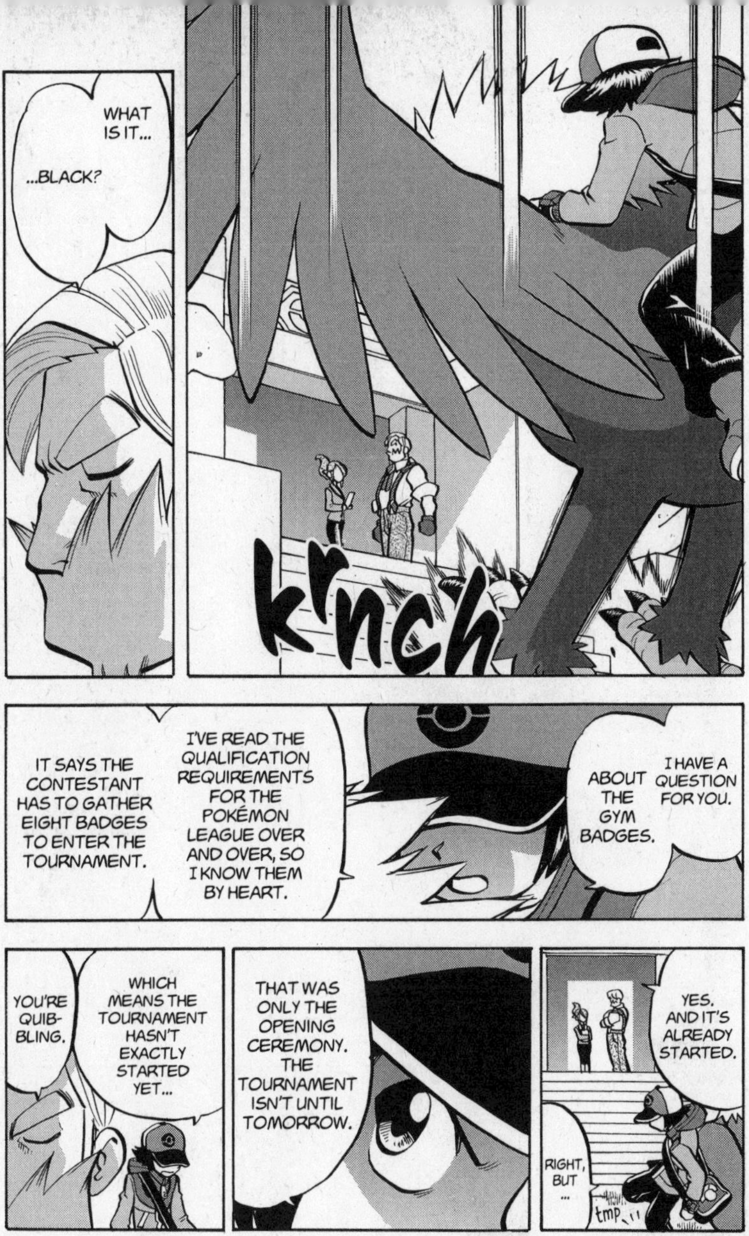
k'nch
WHAT IS IT...
...BLACK?
I HAVE A QUESTION FOR YOU.
ABOUT THE GYM BADGES.
I'VE READ THE QUALIFICATION REQUIREMENTS FOR THE POKÉMON LEAGUE OVER AND OVER, SO I KNOW THEM BY HEART.
IT SAYS THE CONTESTANT HAS TO GATHER EIGHT BADGES TO ENTER THE TOURNAMENT.
YES. AND IT'S ALREADY STARTED.
RIGHT, BUT ...
tmp
THAT WAS ONLY THE OPENING CEREMONY. THE TOURNAMENT ISN'T UNTIL TOMORROW.
WHICH MEANS THE TOURNAMENT HASN'T EXACTLY STARTED YET...
YOU'RE QUIB-BLING.

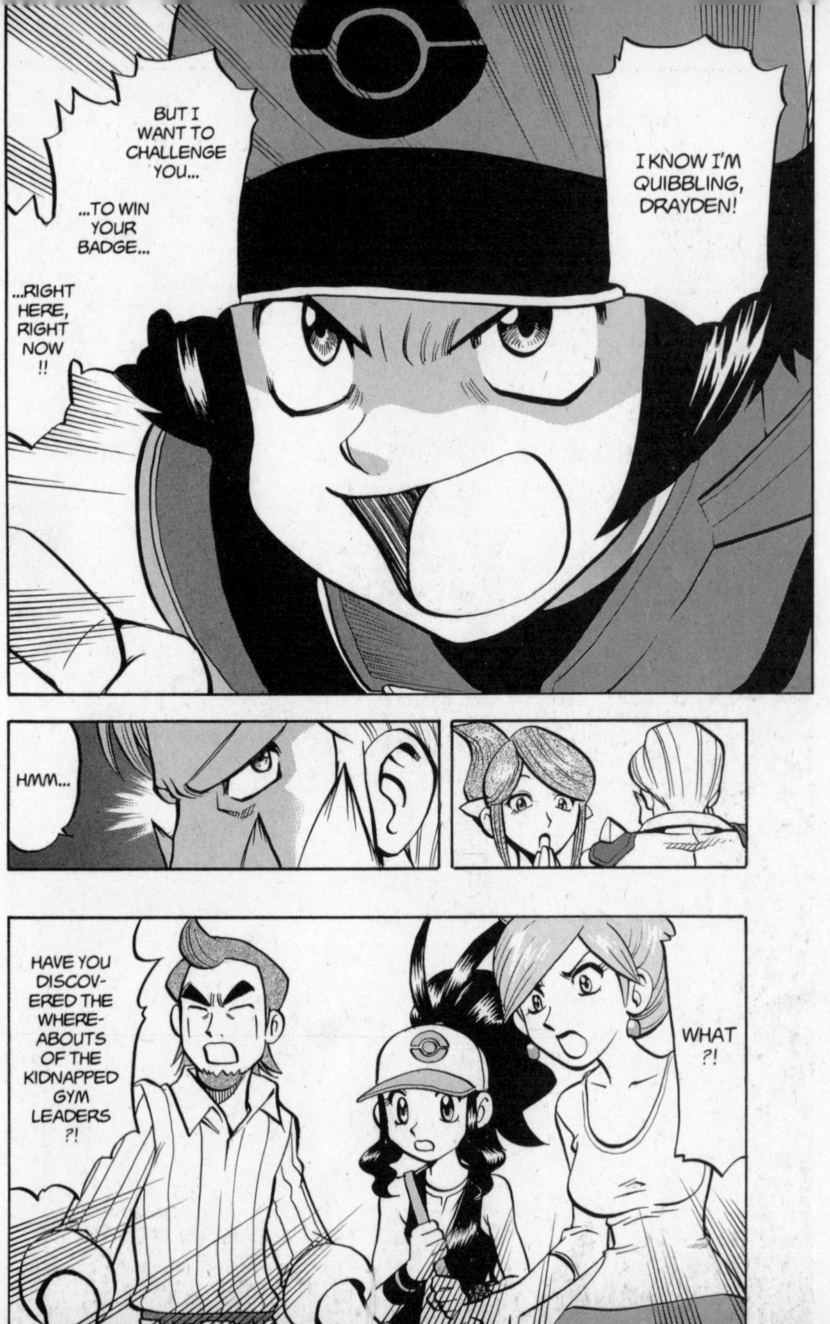
I KNOW I'M QUIBBLING, DRAYDEN!
BUT I WANT TO CHALLENGE YOU...
...TO WIN YOUR BADGE...
...RIGHT HERE, RIGHT NOW!!
HMM...
HAVE YOU DISCOVERED THE WHEREABOUTS OF THE KIDNAPPED GYM LEADERS?!
WHAT?!

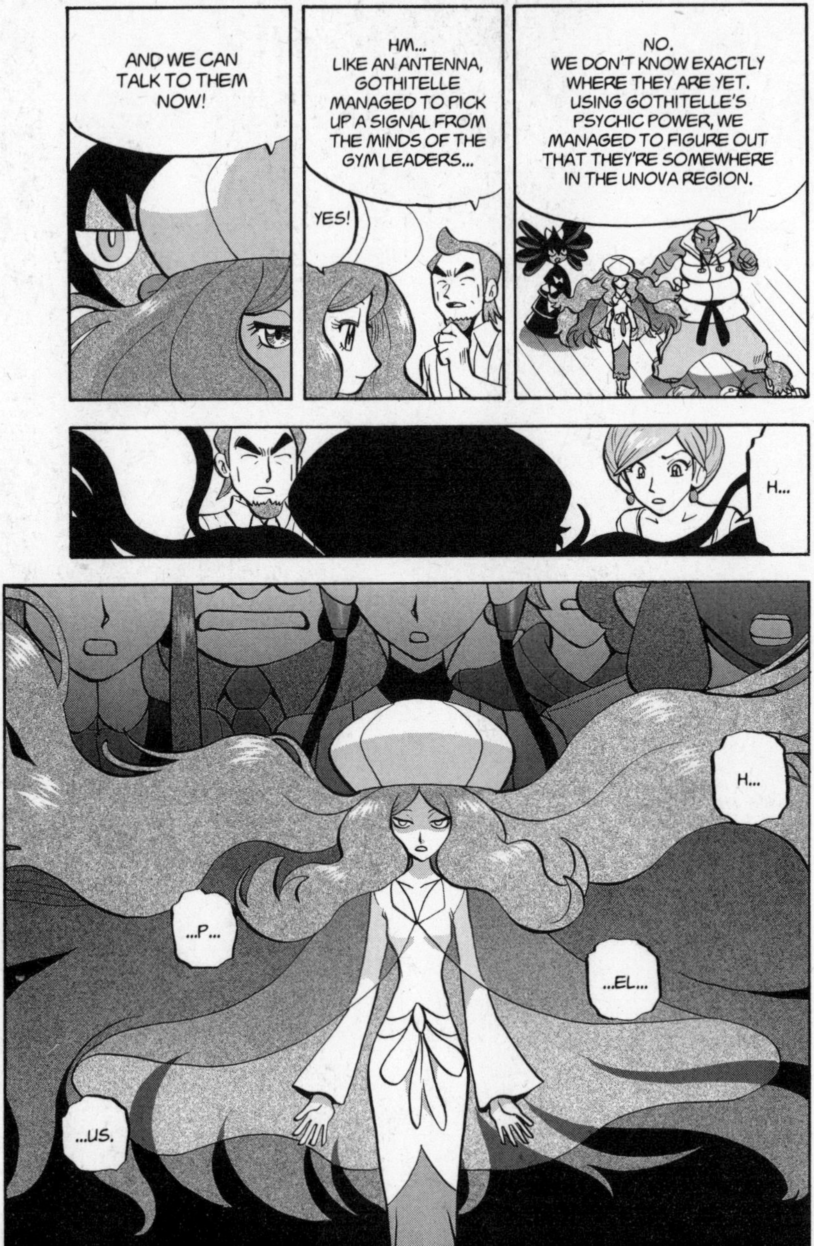
NO.
WE DON'T KNOW EXACTLY WHERE THEY ARE YET. USING GOTHITELLE'S PSYCHIC POWER, WE MANAGED TO FIGURE OUT THAT THEY'RE SOMEWHERE IN THE UNOVA REGION.
HM...
LIKE AN ANTENNA, GOTHITELLE MANAGED TO PICK UP A SIGNAL FROM THE MINDS OF THE GYM LEADERS...
YES!
AND WE CAN TALK TO THEM NOW!
H...
H...
...P...
...EL...
...US.

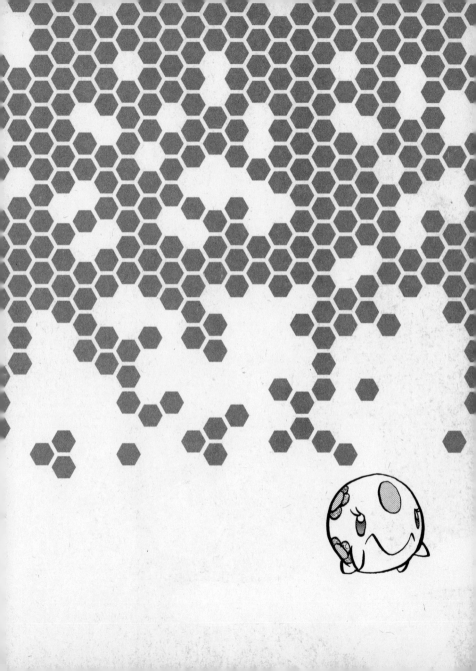

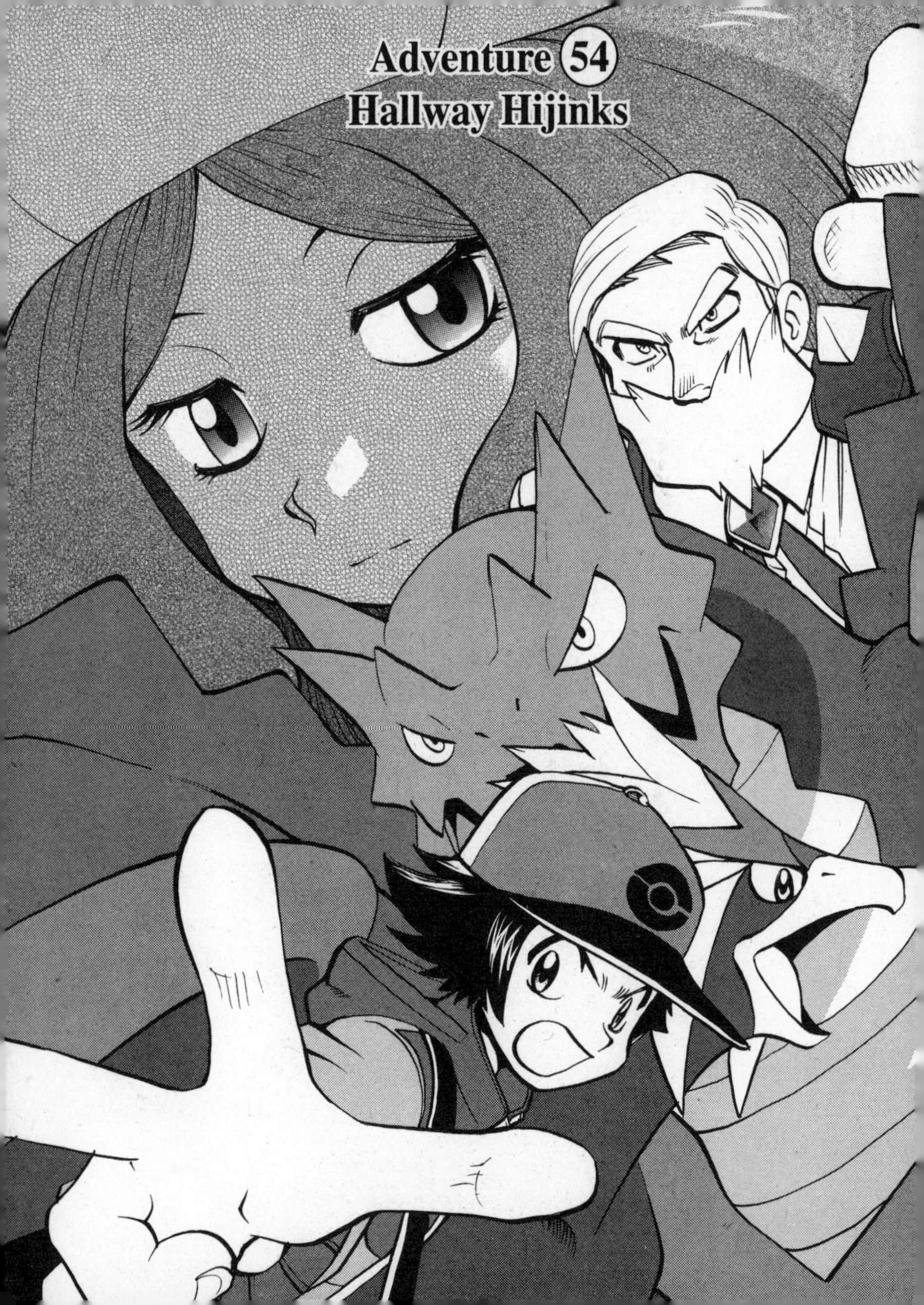
Adventure 54
Hallway Hijinks

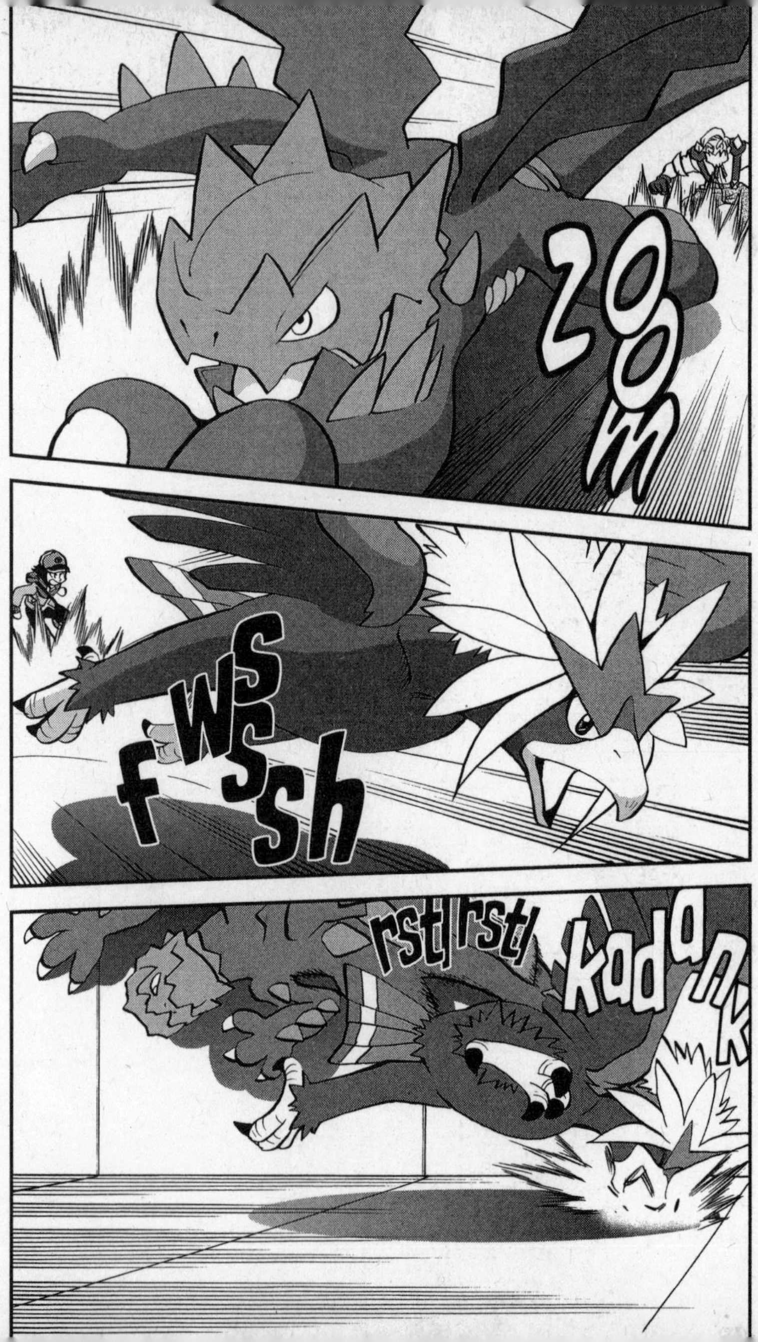
ZOOM
fwssh
rstlrstl
kadank

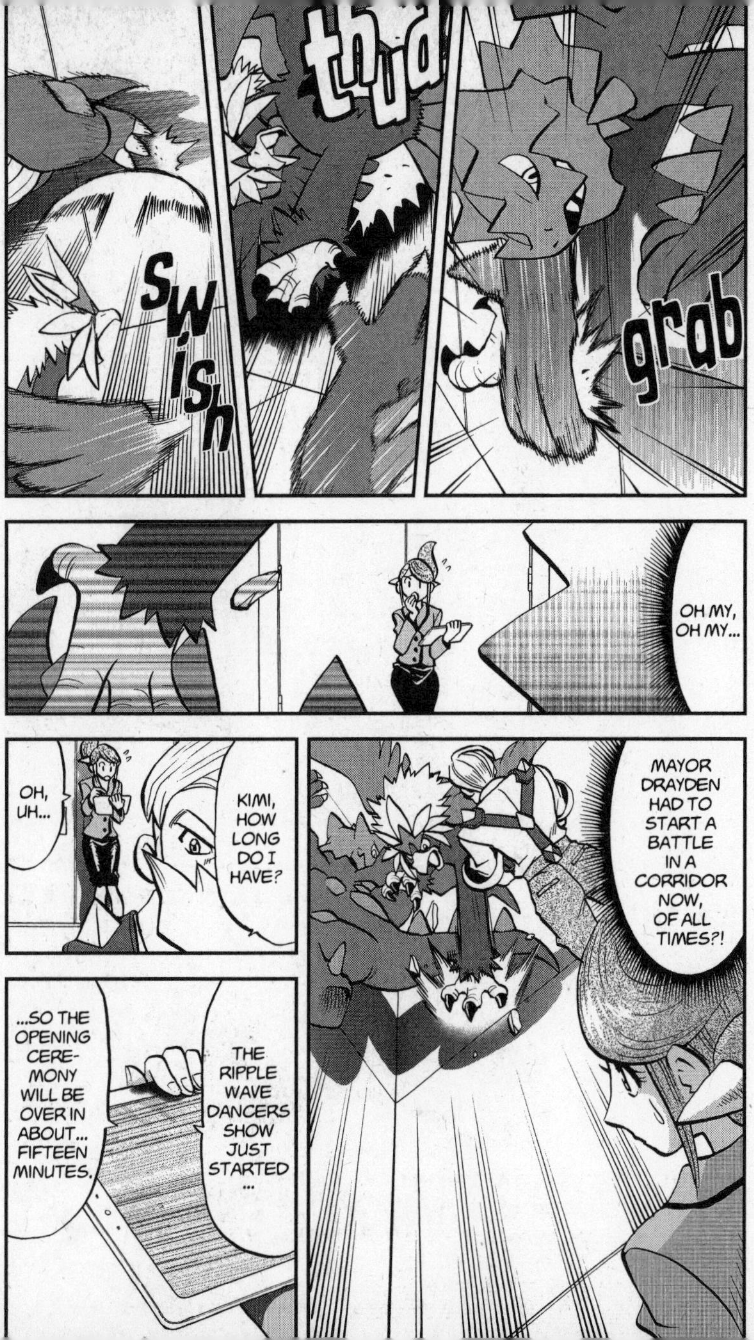
grab
thud
swish
OH MY, OH MY...
MAYOR DRAYDEN HAD TO START A BATTLE IN A CORRIDOR NOW, OF ALL TIMES?!
KIMI, HOW LONG DO I HAVE?
OH, UH...
THE RIPPLE WAVE DANCERS SHOW JUST STARTED...
...SO THE OPENING CEREMONY WILL BE OVER IN ABOUT... FIFTEEN MINUTES.

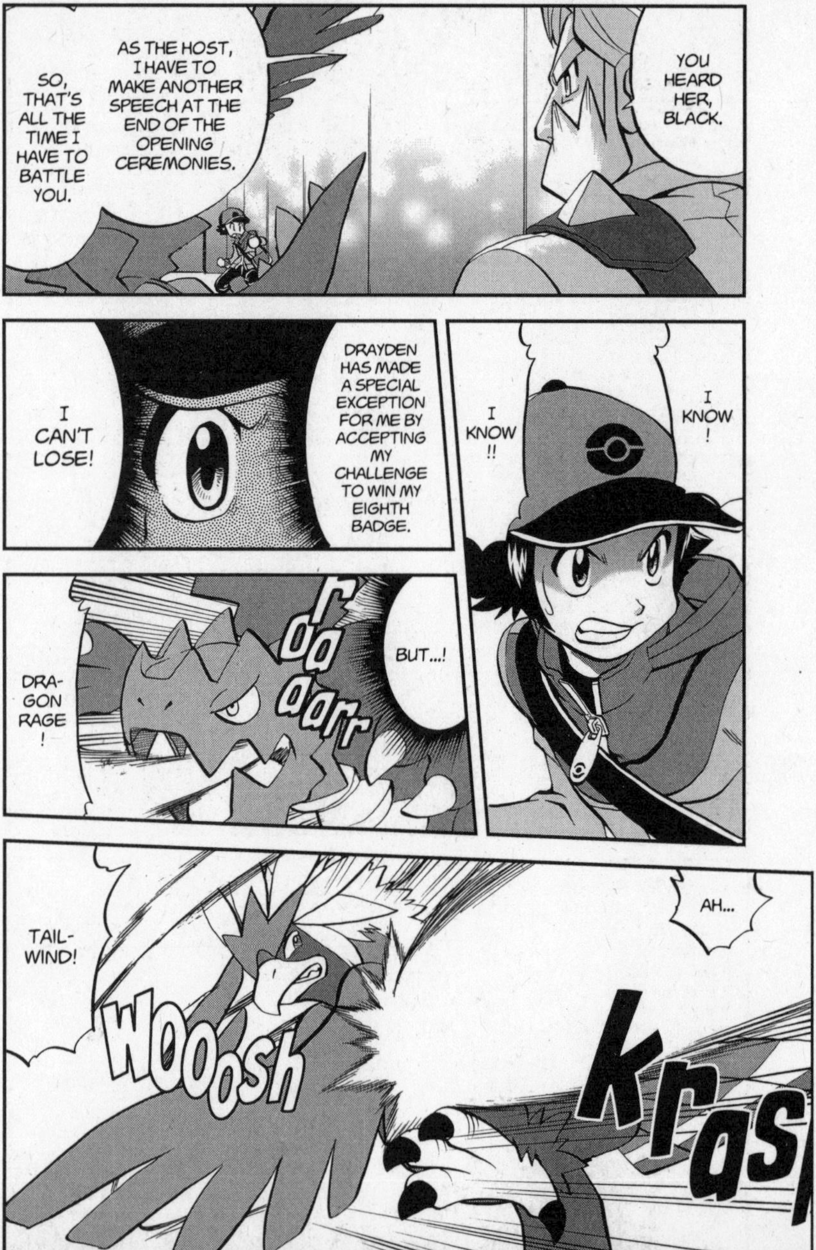
YOU HEARD HER, BLACK.
AS THE HOST, I HAVE TO MAKE ANOTHER SPEECH AT THE END OF THE OPENING CEREMONIES.
SO, THAT'S ALL THE TIME I HAVE TO BATTLE YOU.
I KNOW!
I KNOW!!
BUT...!
DRAYDEN HAS MADE A SPECIAL EXCEPTION FOR ME BY ACCEPTING MY CHALLENGE TO WIN MY EIGHTH BADGE.
I CAN'T LOSE!
roaarr
DRA-GON RAGE!
AH...
TAIL-WIND!
WOOOsh
kras

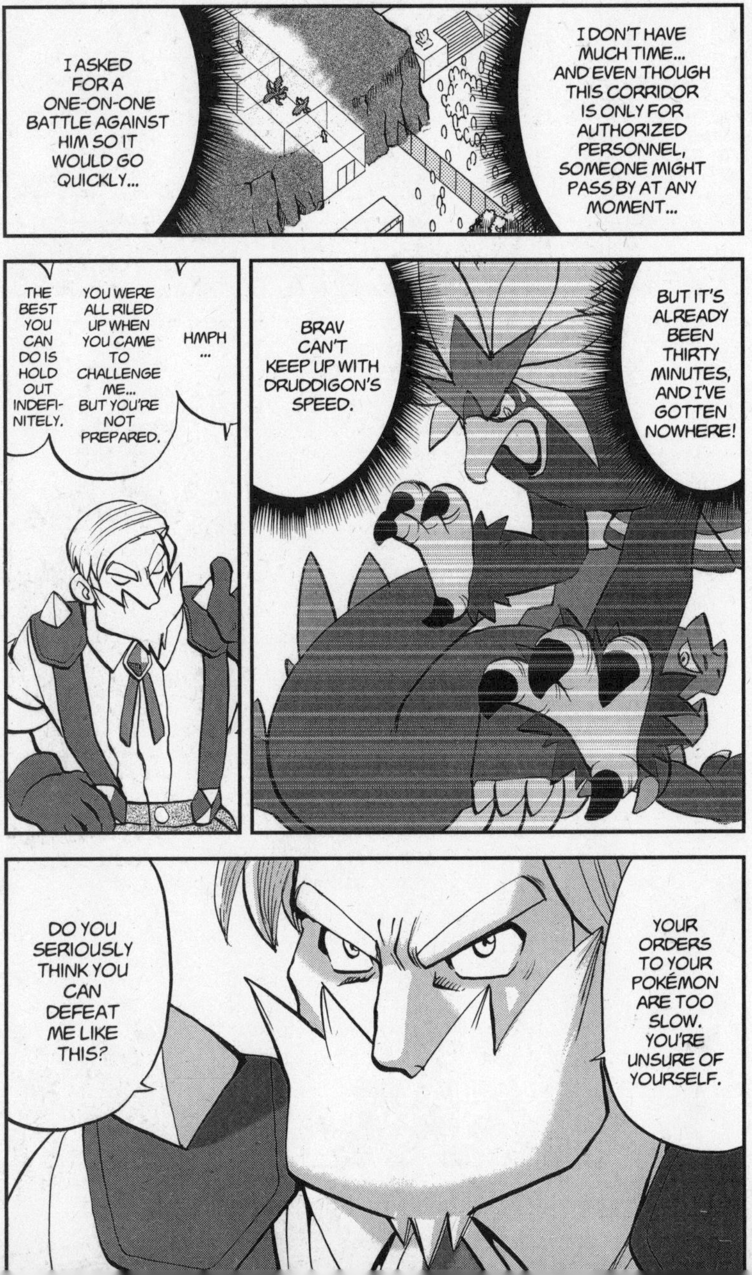
I DON'T HAVE MUCH TIME... AND EVEN THOUGH THIS CORRIDOR IS ONLY FOR AUTHORIZED PERSONNEL, SOMEONE MIGHT PASS BY AT ANY MOMENT...
I ASKED FOR A ONE-ON-ONE BATTLE AGAINST HIM SO IT WOULD GO QUICKLY...
BUT IT'S ALREADY BEEN THIRTY MINUTES, AND I'VE GOTTEN NOWHERE!
BRAV CAN'T KEEP UP WITH DRUDDIGON'S SPEED.
HMPH...
YOU WERE ALL RILED UP WHEN YOU CAME TO CHALLENGE ME... BUT YOU'RE NOT PREPARED.
THE BEST YOU CAN DO IS HOLD OUT INDEFINITELY.
YOUR ORDERS TO YOUR POKÉMON ARE TOO SLOW. YOU'RE UNSURE OF YOURSELF.
DO YOU SERIOUSLY THINK YOU CAN DEFEAT ME LIKE THIS?

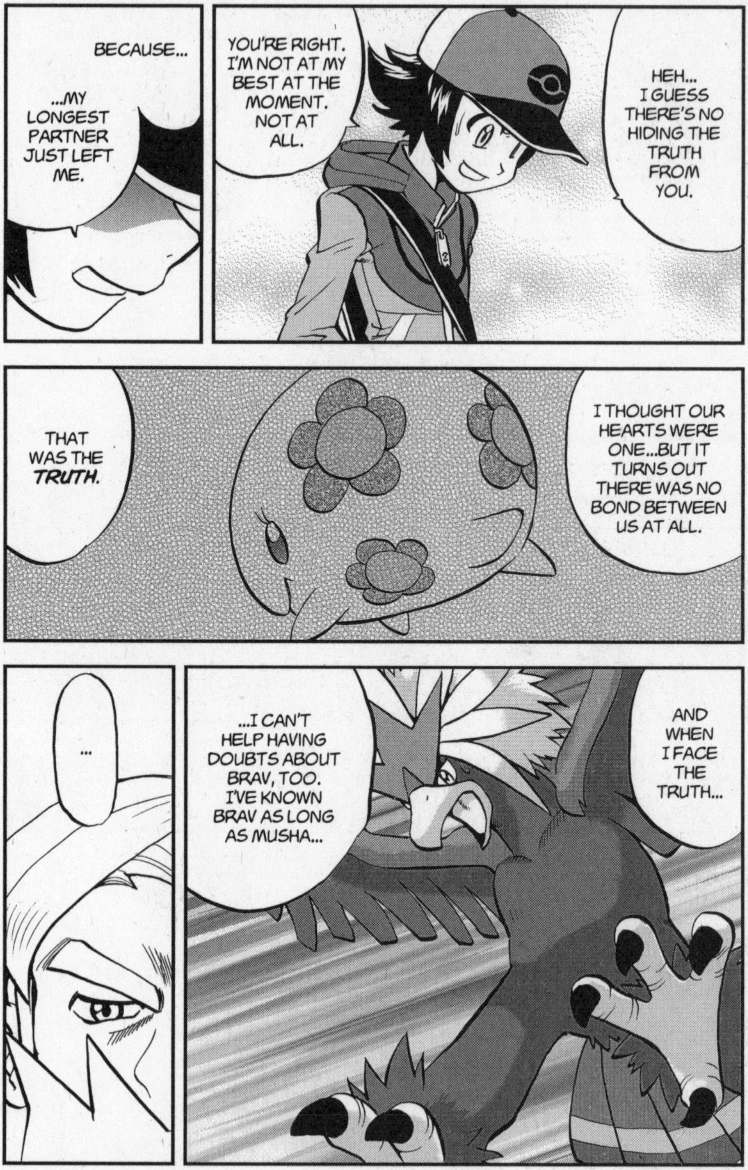
HEH... I GUESS THERE'S NO HIDING THE TRUTH FROM YOU.
YOU'RE RIGHT. I'M NOT AT MY BEST AT THE MOMENT. NOT AT ALL.
BECAUSE...
...MY LONGEST PARTNER JUST LEFT ME.
I THOUGHT OUR HEARTS WERE ONE...BUT IT TURNS OUT THERE WAS NO BOND BETWEEN US AT ALL.
THAT WAS THE *TRUTH*.
AND WHEN I FACE THE TRUTH...
...I CAN'T HELP HAVING DOUBTS ABOUT BRAV, TOO. I'VE KNOWN BRAV AS LONG AS MUSHA...
...

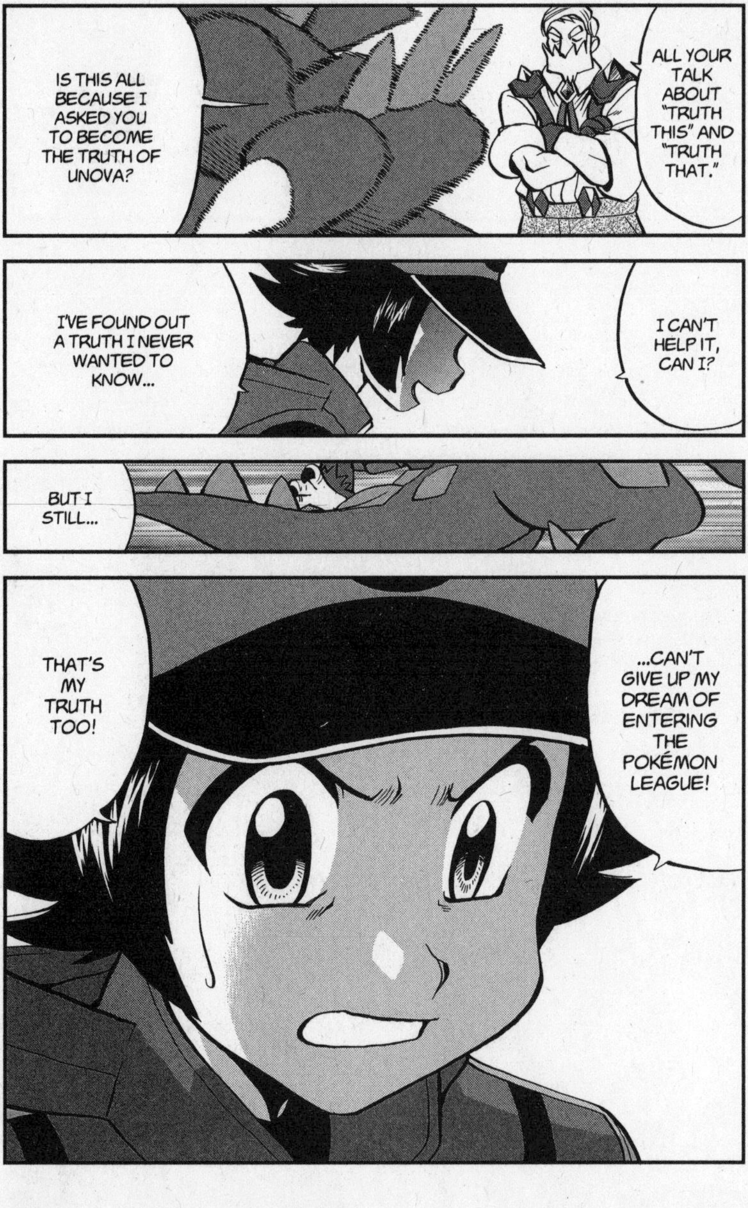
ALL YOUR TALK ABOUT "TRUTH THIS" AND "TRUTH THAT."
IS THIS ALL BECAUSE I ASKED YOU TO BECOME THE TRUTH OF UNOVA?
I CAN'T HELP IT, CAN I?
I'VE FOUND OUT A TRUTH I NEVER WANTED TO KNOW...
BUT I STILL...
...CAN'T GIVE UP MY DREAM OF ENTERING THE POKÉMON LEAGUE!
THAT'S MY TRUTH TOO!

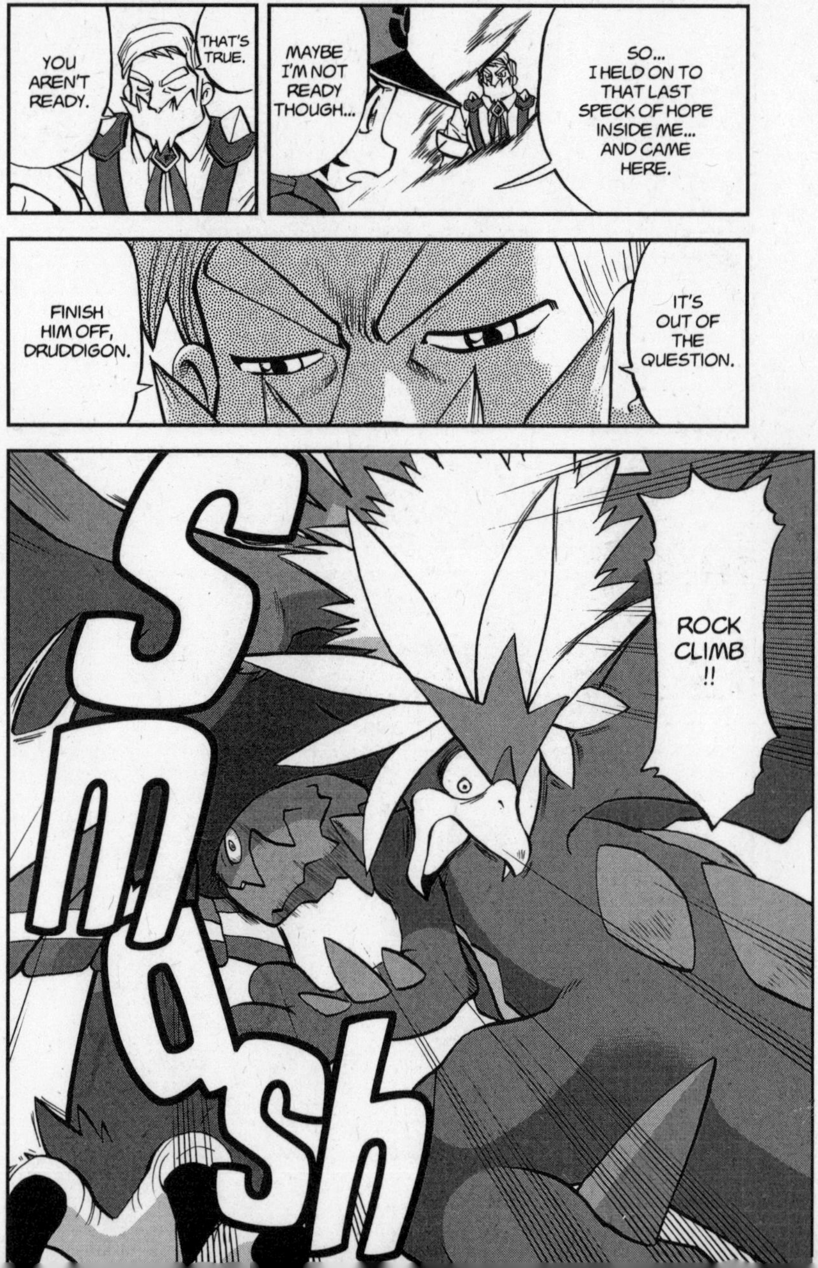
SO... I HELD ON TO THAT LAST SPECK OF HOPE INSIDE ME... AND CAME HERE.
MAYBE I'M NOT READY THOUGH...
THAT'S TRUE.
YOU AREN'T READY.
IT'S OUT OF THE QUESTION.
FINISH HIM OFF, DRUDDIGON.
ROCK CLIMB !!
Smash

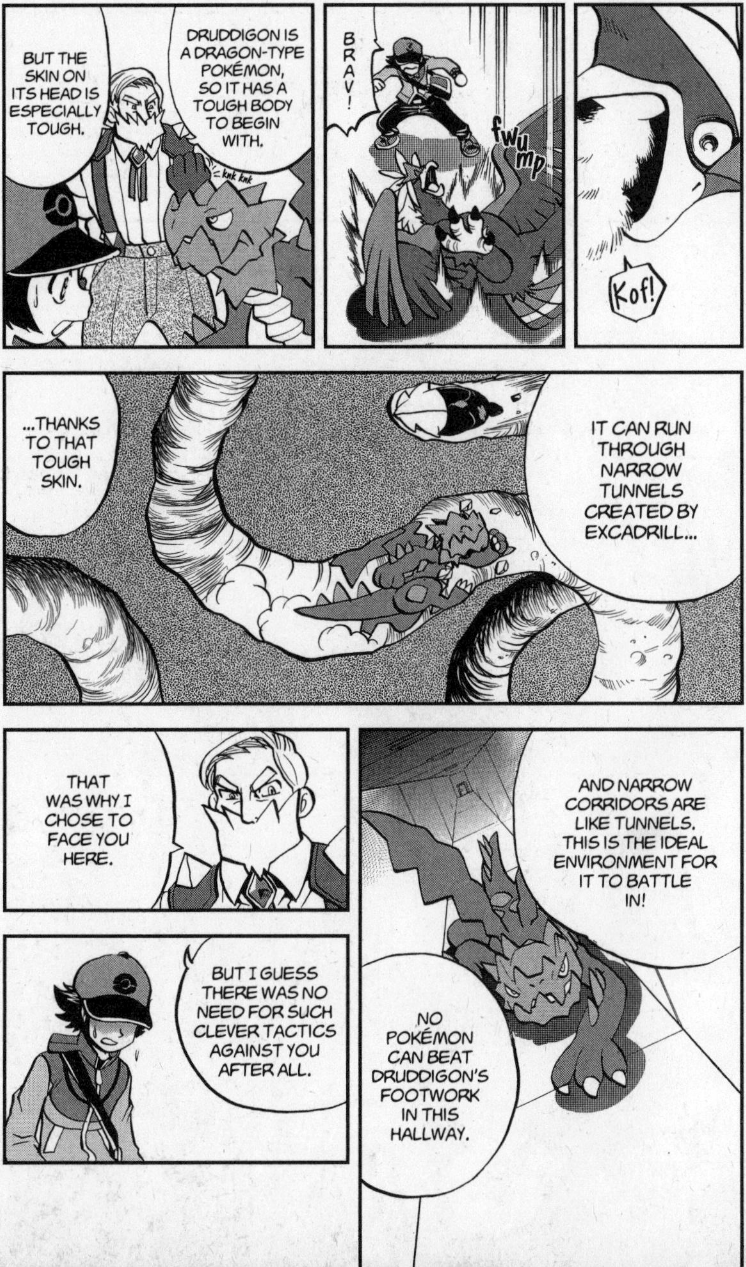
Kof!
BRAV!
fwump
DRUDDIGON IS A DRAGON-TYPE POKÉMON, SO IT HAS A TOUGH BODY TO BEGIN WITH.
knk knk
BUT THE SKIN ON ITS HEAD IS ESPECIALLY TOUGH.
IT CAN RUN THROUGH NARROW TUNNELS CREATED BY EXCADRILL...
...THANKS TO THAT TOUGH SKIN.
AND NARROW CORRIDORS ARE LIKE TUNNELS. THIS IS THE IDEAL ENVIRONMENT FOR IT TO BATTLE IN!
NO POKÉMON CAN BEAT DRUDDIGON'S FOOTWORK IN THIS HALLWAY.
THAT WAS WHY I CHOSE TO FACE YOU HERE.
BUT I GUESS THERE WAS NO NEED FOR SUCH CLEVER TACTICS AGAINST YOU AFTER ALL.

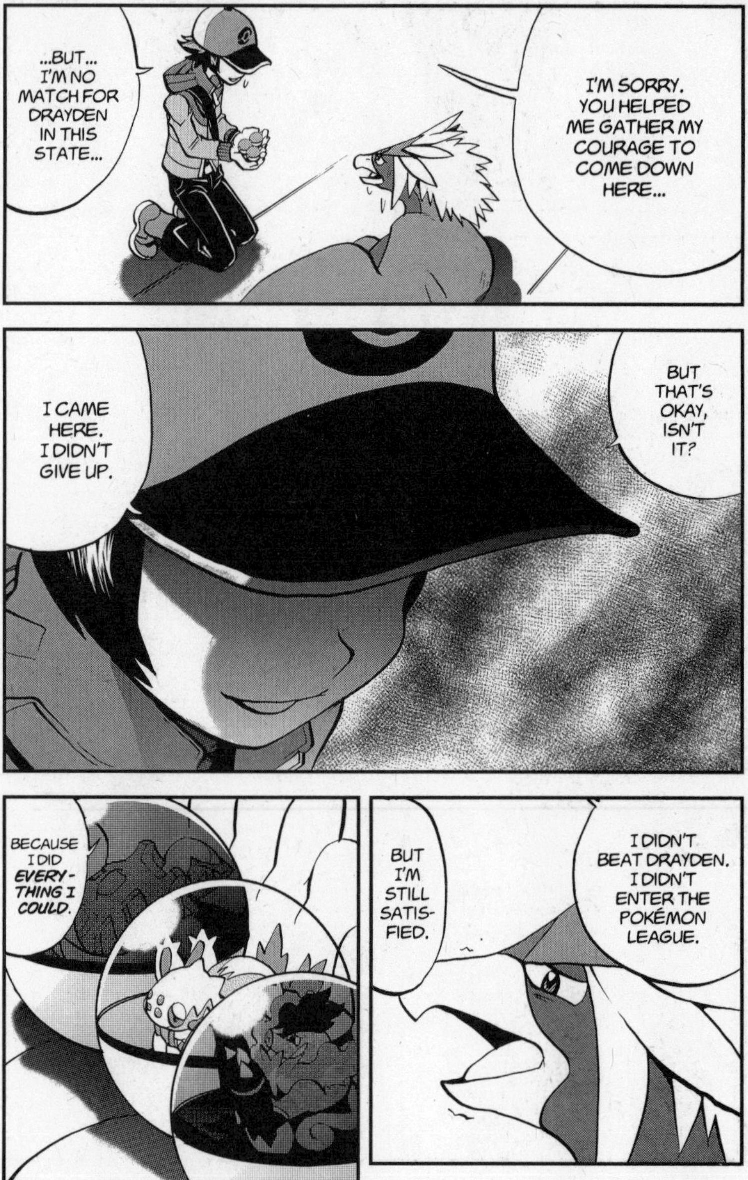
I'M SORRY. YOU HELPED ME GATHER MY COURAGE TO COME DOWN HERE...
...BUT... I'M NO MATCH FOR DRAYDEN IN THIS STATE...
BUT THAT'S OKAY, ISN'T IT?
I CAME HERE. I DIDN'T GIVE UP.
I DIDN'T BEAT DRAYDEN. I DIDN'T ENTER THE POKÉMON LEAGUE.
BUT I'M STILL SATIS-FIED.
BECAUSE I DID ***EVERY-THING I COULD.***

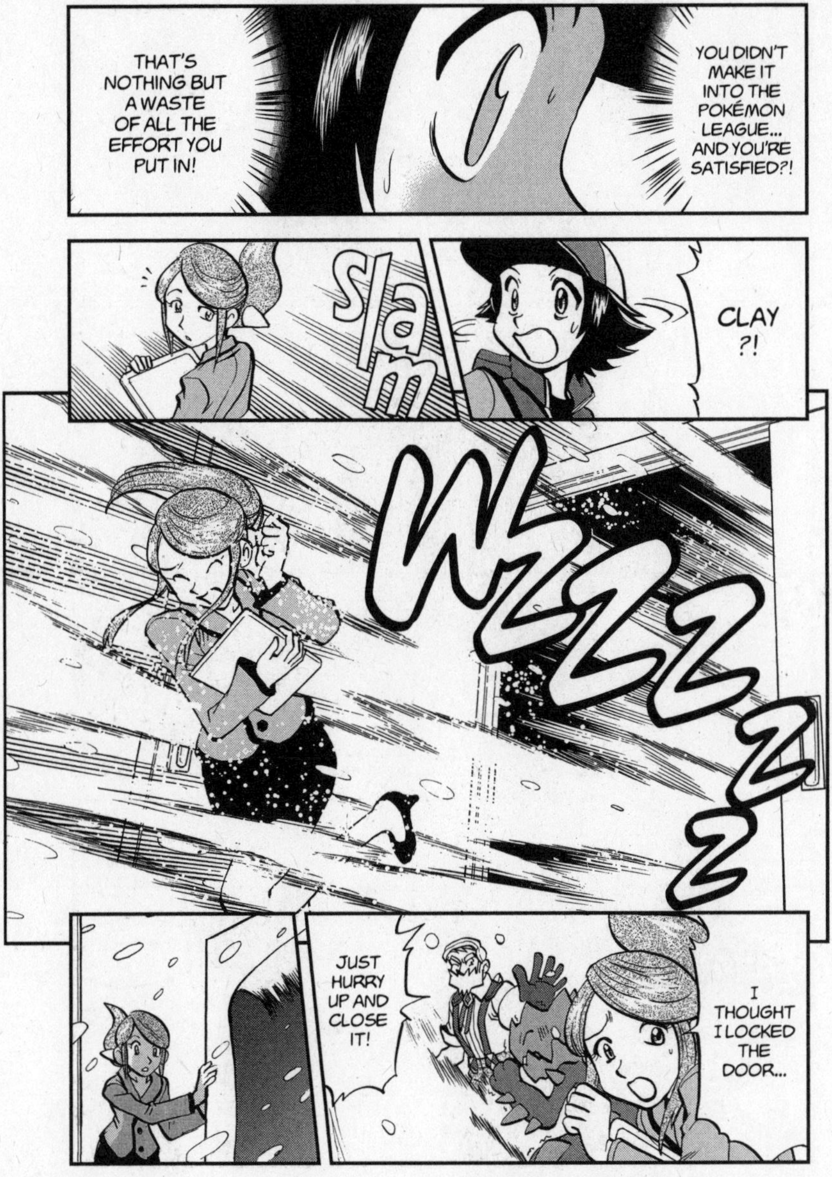
YOU DIDN'T MAKE IT INTO THE POKÉMON LEAGUE... AND YOU'RE SATISFIED?!
THAT'S NOTHING BUT A WASTE OF ALL THE EFFORT YOU PUT IN!
CLAY ?!
slam
WZZZZZZ
I THOUGHT I LOCKED THE DOOR...
JUST HURRY UP AND CLOSE IT!

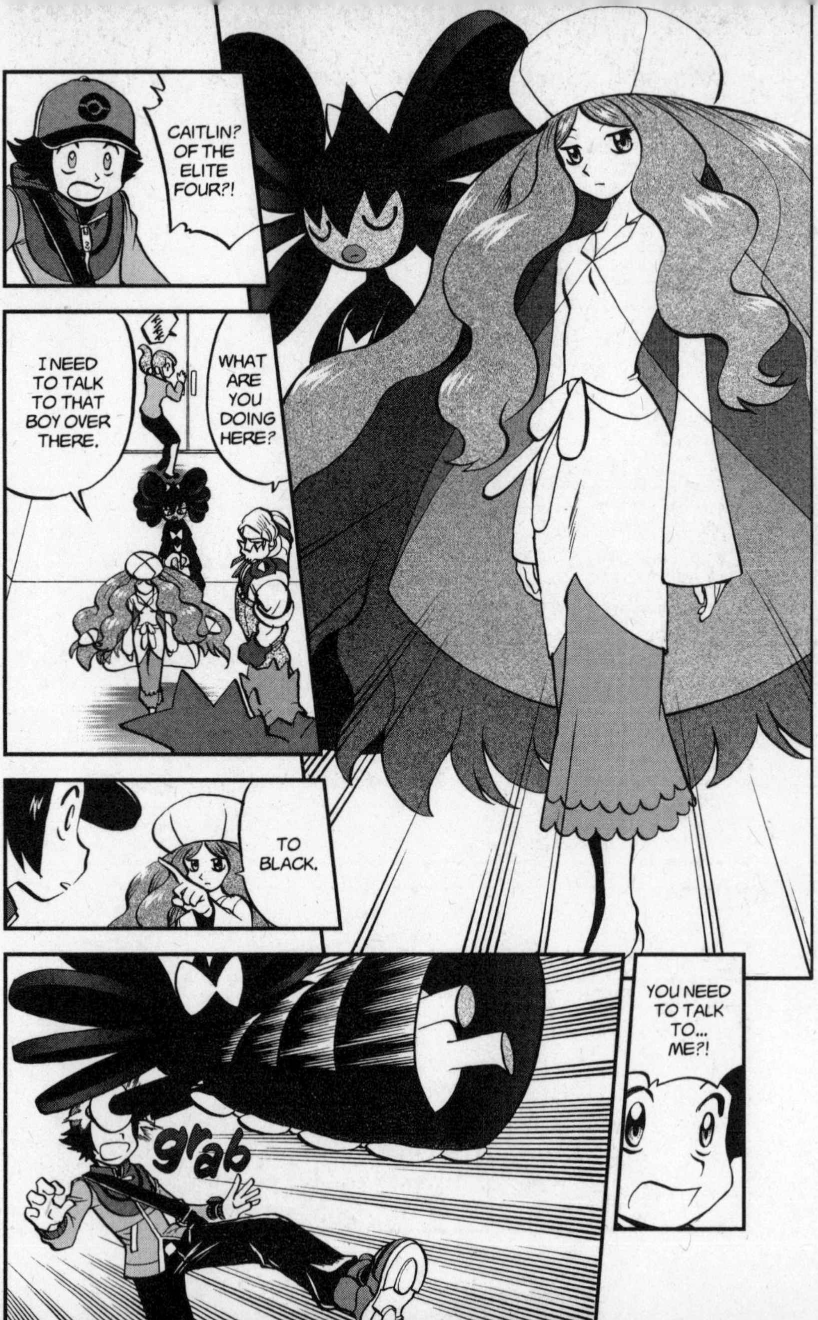
CAITLIN? OF THE ELITE FOUR?!
WHAT ARE YOU DOING HERE?
I NEED TO TALK TO THAT BOY OVER THERE.
TO BLACK.
YOU NEED TO TALK TO... ME?!
grab

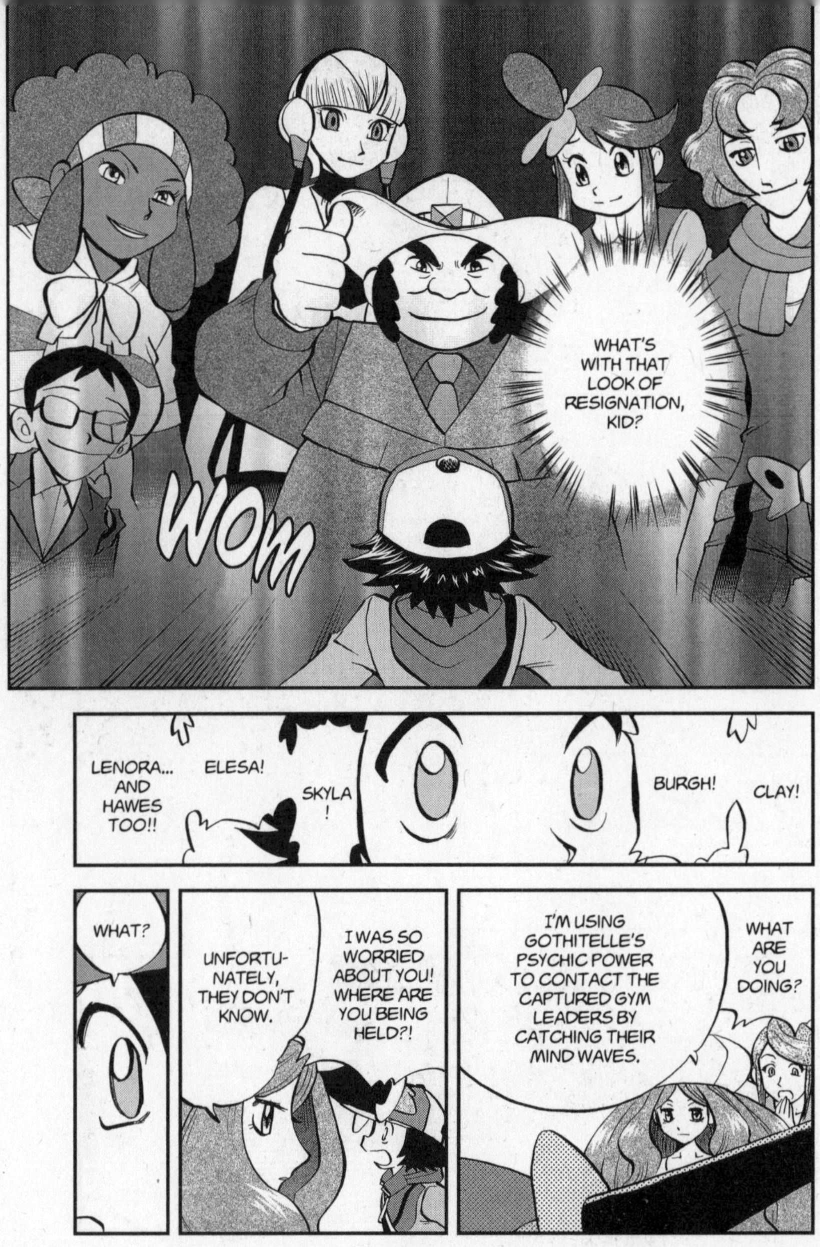
WHAT'S WITH THAT LOOK OF RESIGNATION, KID?
WOM
CLAY!
BURGH!
SKYLA!
ELESA!
LENORA... AND HAWES TOO!!
WHAT ARE YOU DOING?
I'M USING GOTHITELLE'S PSYCHIC POWER TO CONTACT THE CAPTURED GYM LEADERS BY CATCHING THEIR MIND WAVES.
I WAS SO WORRIED ABOUT YOU! WHERE ARE YOU BEING HELD?!
UNFORTU-NATELY, THEY DON'T KNOW.
WHAT?

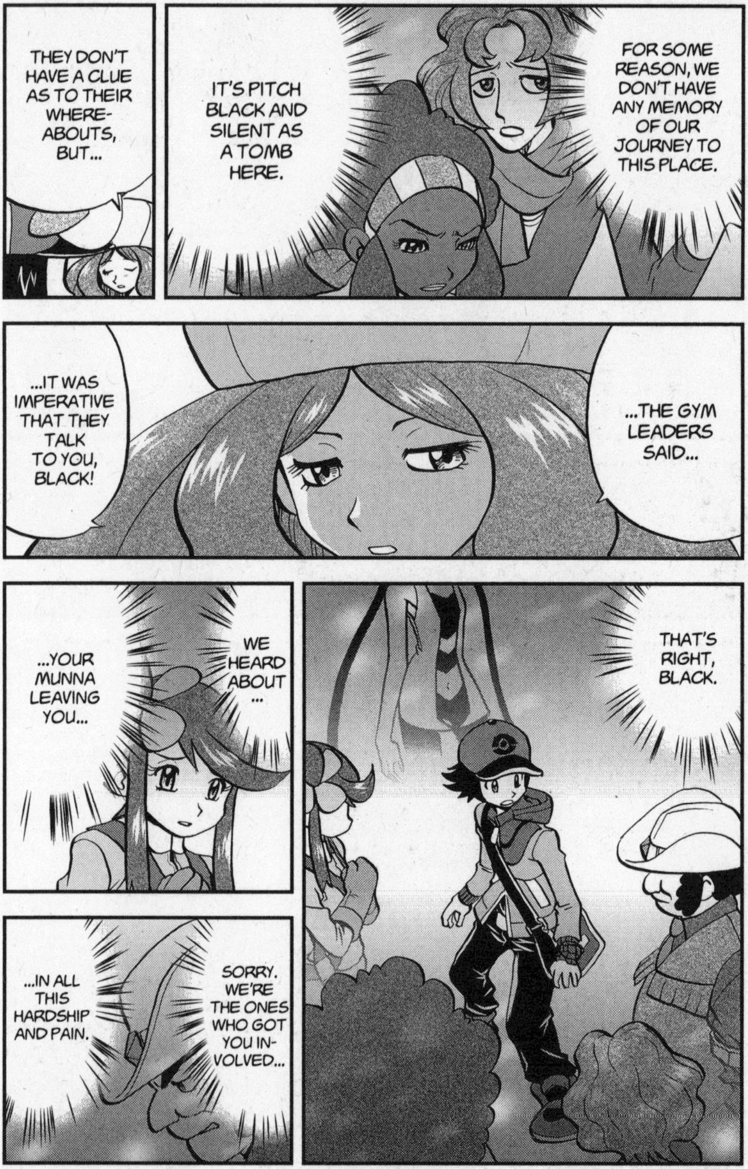
FOR SOME REASON, WE DON'T HAVE ANY MEMORY OF OUR JOURNEY TO THIS PLACE.
IT'S PITCH BLACK AND SILENT AS A TOMB HERE.
THEY DON'T HAVE A CLUE AS TO THEIR WHERE-ABOUTS, BUT...
...THE GYM LEADERS SAID...
...IT WAS IMPERATIVE THAT THEY TALK TO YOU, BLACK!
THAT'S RIGHT, BLACK.
WE HEARD ABOUT ...
...YOUR MUNNA LEAVING YOU...
SORRY. WE'RE THE ONES WHO GOT YOU IN-VOLVED...
...IN ALL THIS HARDSHIP AND PAIN.

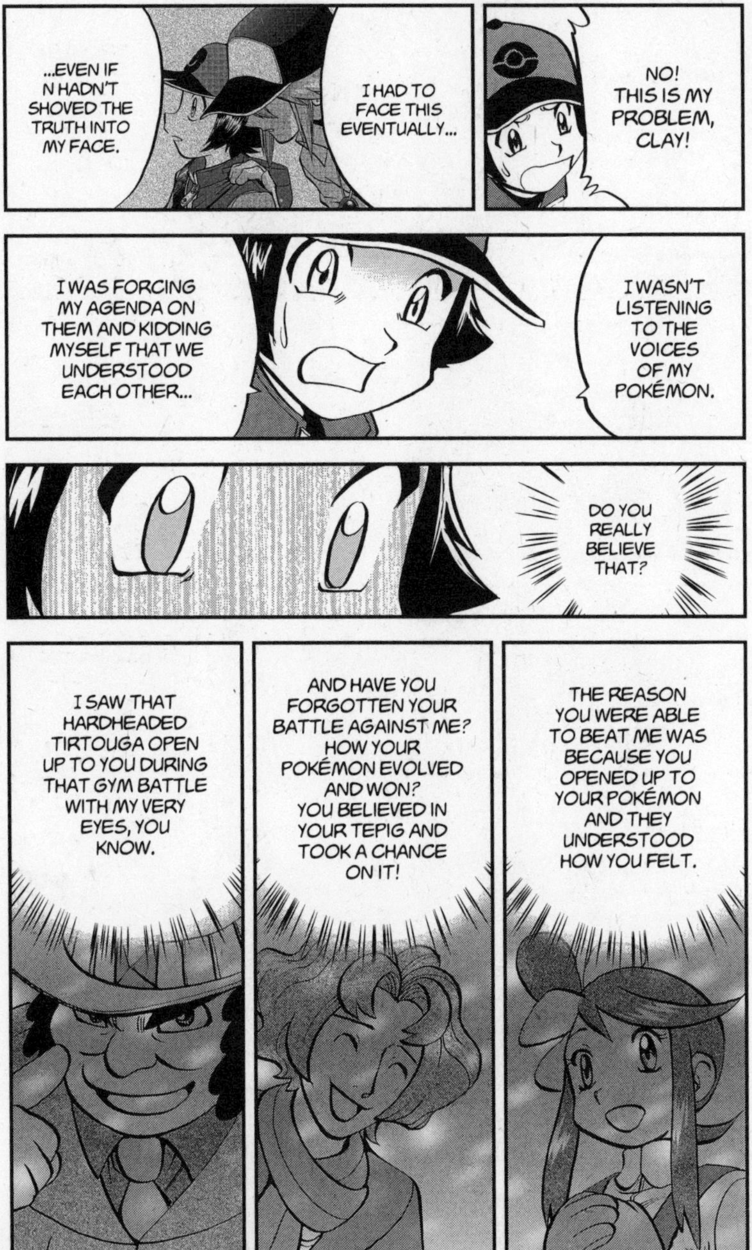
NO! THIS IS MY PROBLEM, CLAY!
I HAD TO FACE THIS EVENTUALLY...
...EVEN IF N HADN'T SHOVED THE TRUTH INTO MY FACE.
I WASN'T LISTENING TO THE VOICES OF MY POKÉMON.
I WAS FORCING MY AGENDA ON THEM AND KIDDING MYSELF THAT WE UNDERSTOOD EACH OTHER...
DO YOU REALLY BELIEVE THAT?
THE REASON YOU WERE ABLE TO BEAT ME WAS BECAUSE YOU OPENED UP TO YOUR POKÉMON AND THEY UNDERSTOOD HOW YOU FELT.
AND HAVE YOU FORGOTTEN YOUR BATTLE AGAINST ME? HOW YOUR POKÉMON EVOLVED AND WON? YOU BELIEVED IN YOUR TEPIG AND TOOK A CHANCE ON IT!
I SAW THAT HARDHEADED TIRTOUGA OPEN UP TO YOU DURING THAT GYM BATTLE WITH MY VERY EYES, YOU KNOW.

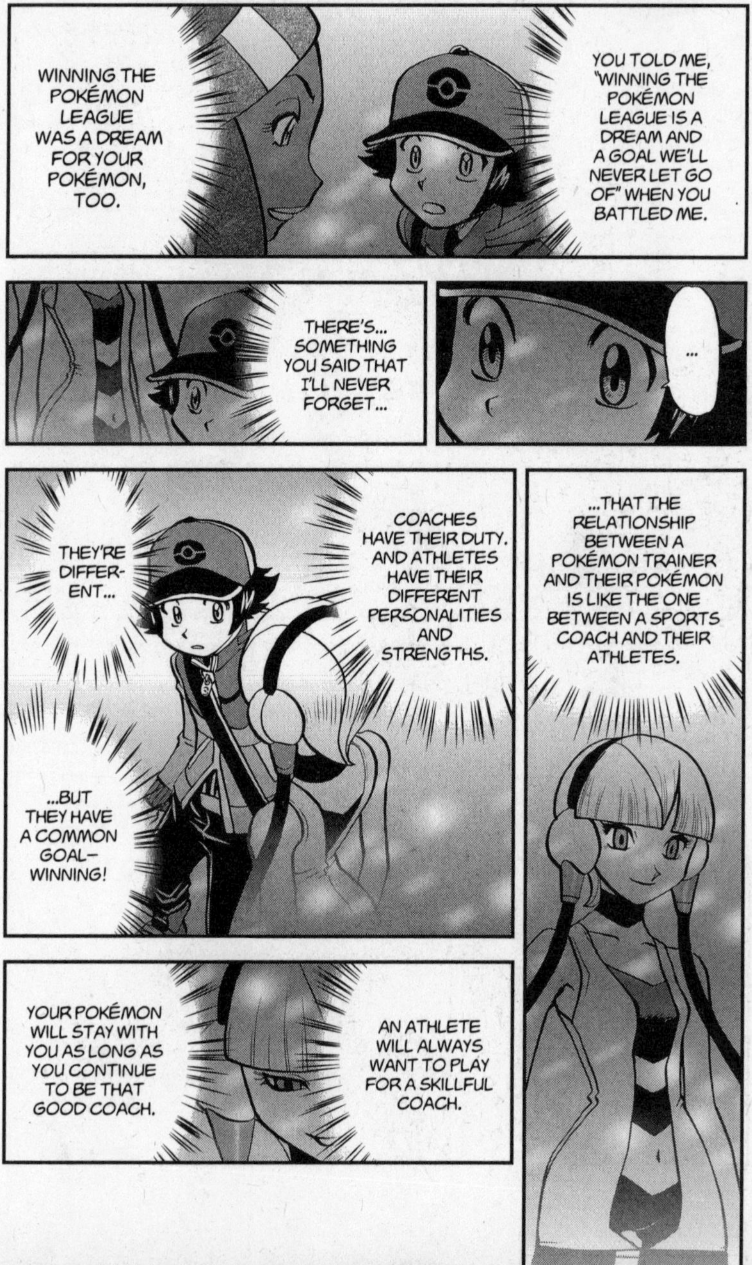
YOU TOLD ME, "WINNING THE POKÉMON LEAGUE IS A DREAM AND A GOAL WE'LL NEVER LET GO OF" WHEN YOU BATTLED ME.
WINNING THE POKÉMON LEAGUE WAS A DREAM FOR YOUR POKÉMON, TOO.
...
THERE'S... SOMETHING YOU SAID THAT I'LL NEVER FORGET...
...THAT THE RELATIONSHIP BETWEEN A POKÉMON TRAINER AND THEIR POKÉMON IS LIKE THE ONE BETWEEN A SPORTS COACH AND THEIR ATHLETES.
COACHES HAVE THEIR DUTY. AND ATHLETES HAVE THEIR DIFFERENT PERSONALITIES AND STRENGTHS.
THEY'RE DIFFER-ENT...
...BUT THEY HAVE A COMMON GOAL—WINNING!
AN ATHLETE WILL ALWAYS WANT TO PLAY FOR A SKILLFUL COACH.
YOUR POKÉMON WILL STAY WITH YOU AS LONG AS YOU CONTINUE TO BE THAT GOOD COACH.

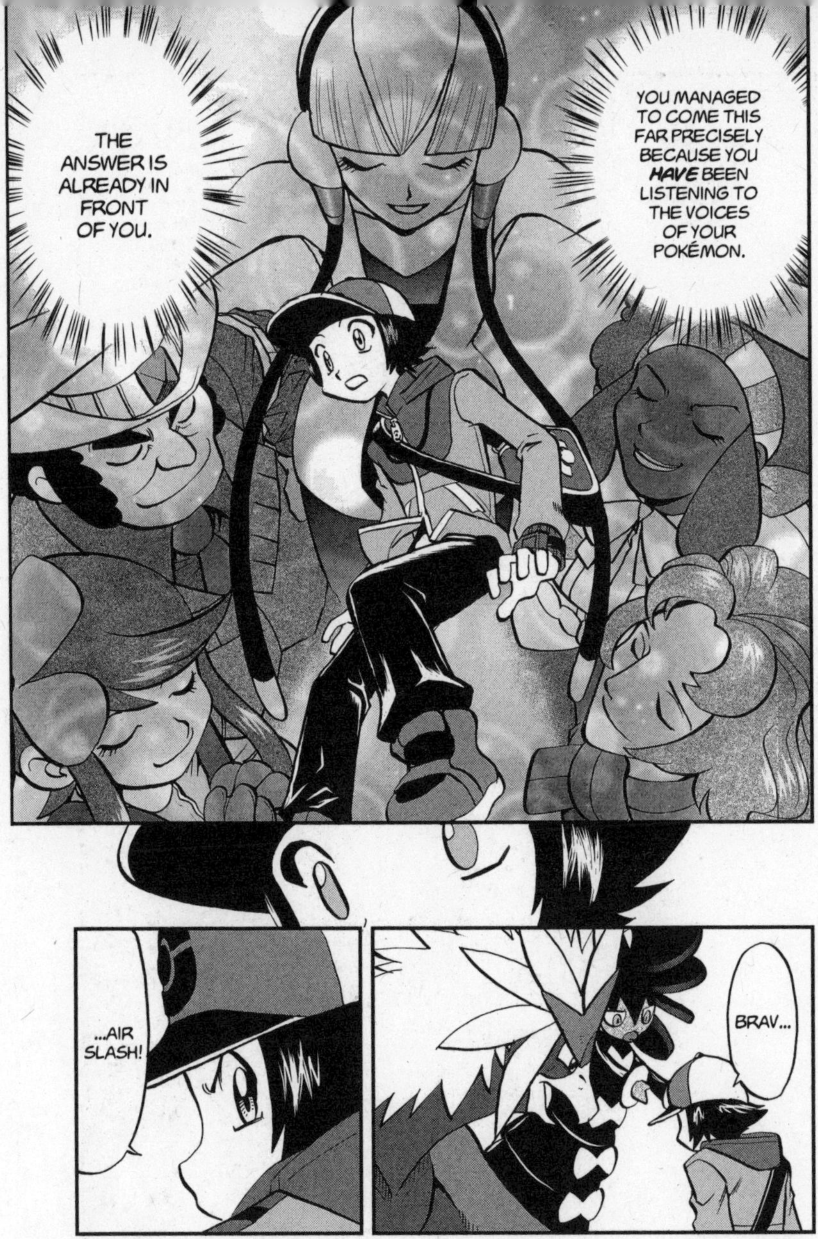
YOU MANAGED TO COME THIS FAR PRECISELY BECAUSE YOU **HAVE** BEEN LISTENING TO THE VOICES OF YOUR POKÉMON.
THE ANSWER IS ALREADY IN FRONT OF YOU.
BRAV...
...AIR SLASH!

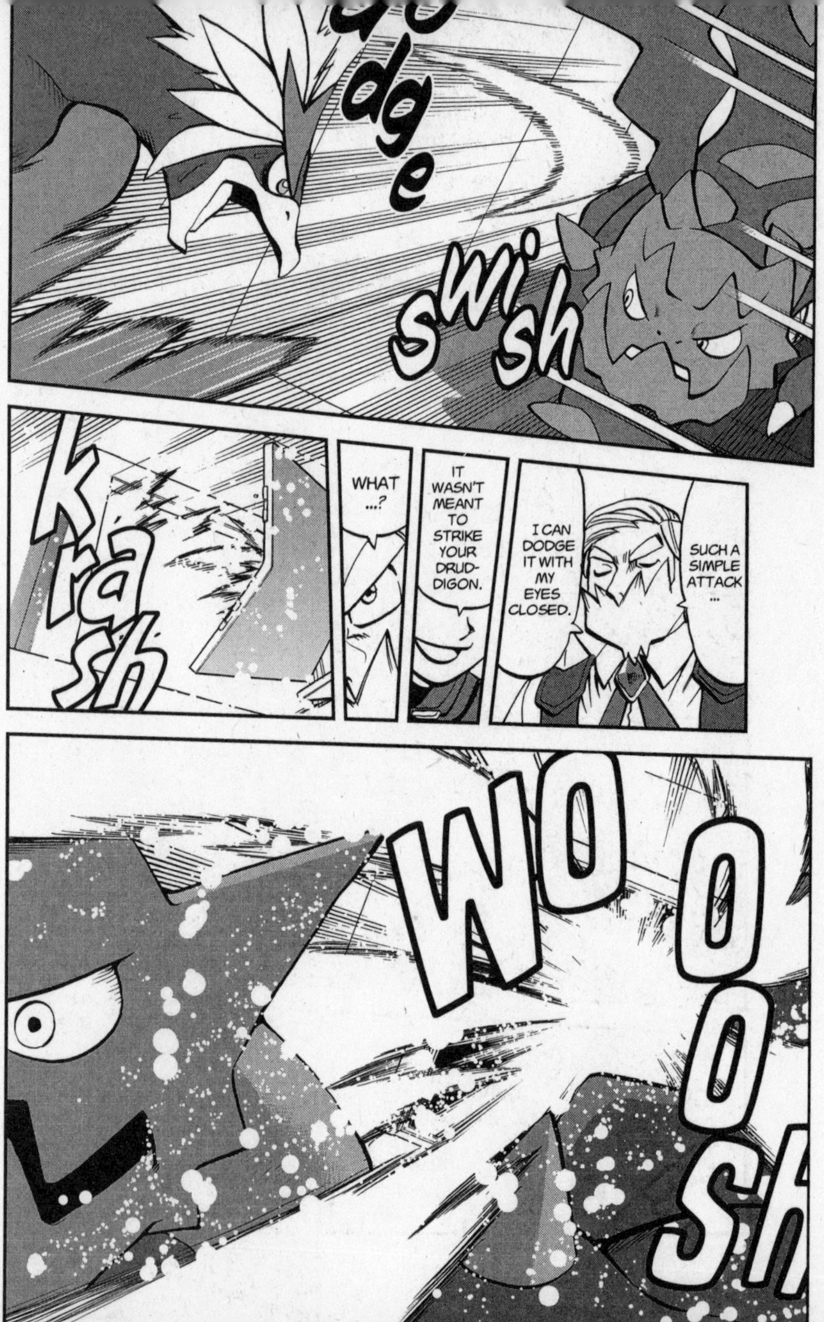
dge
swish
SUCH A SIMPLE ATTACK ...
I CAN DODGE IT WITH MY EYES CLOSED.
IT WASN'T MEANT TO STRIKE YOUR DRUD-DIGON.
WHAT ...?
krash
WOOOOSh

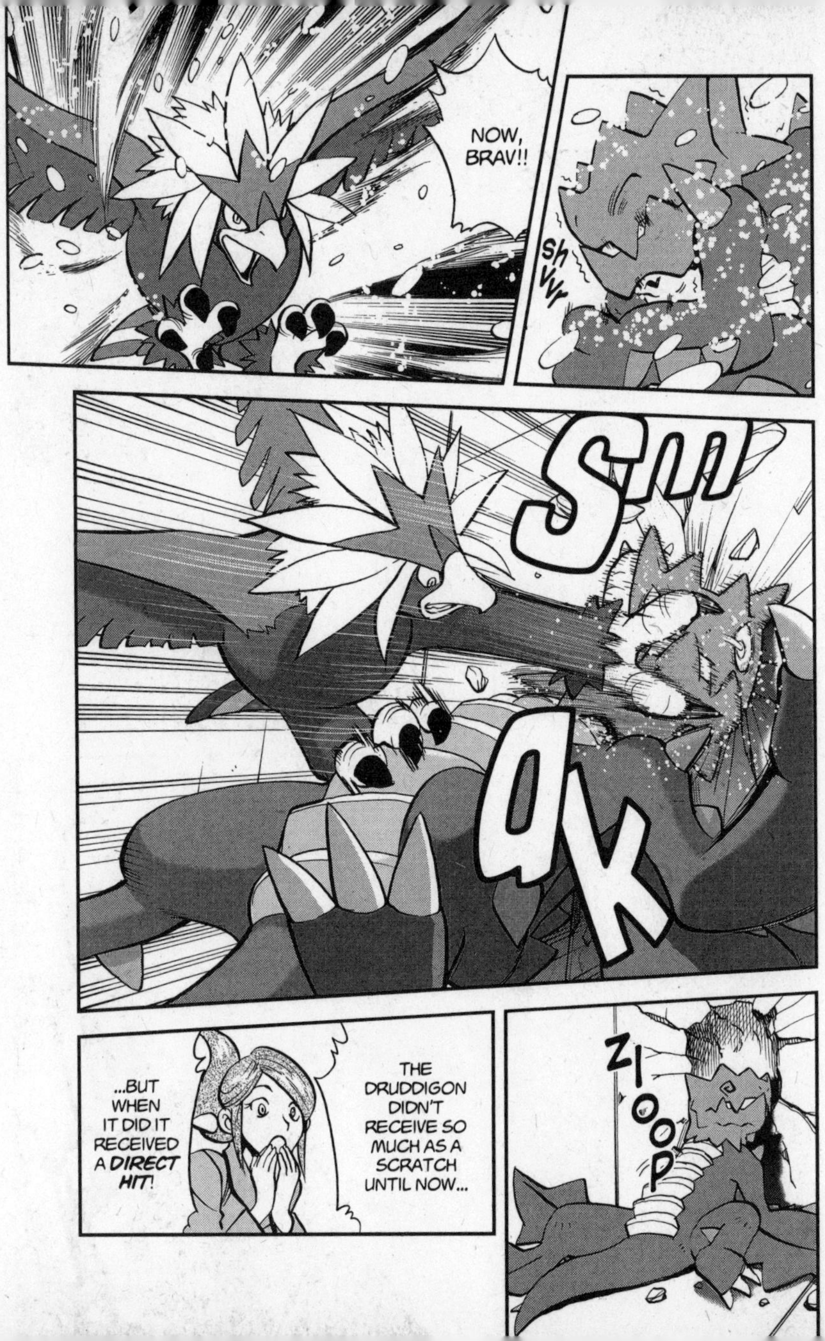
shvvr
NOW, BRAV!!
SMACK
ZIOOP
THE DRUDDIGON DIDN'T RECEIVE SO MUCH AS A SCRATCH UNTIL NOW...
...BUT WHEN IT DID IT RECEIVED A **DIRECT HIT**!

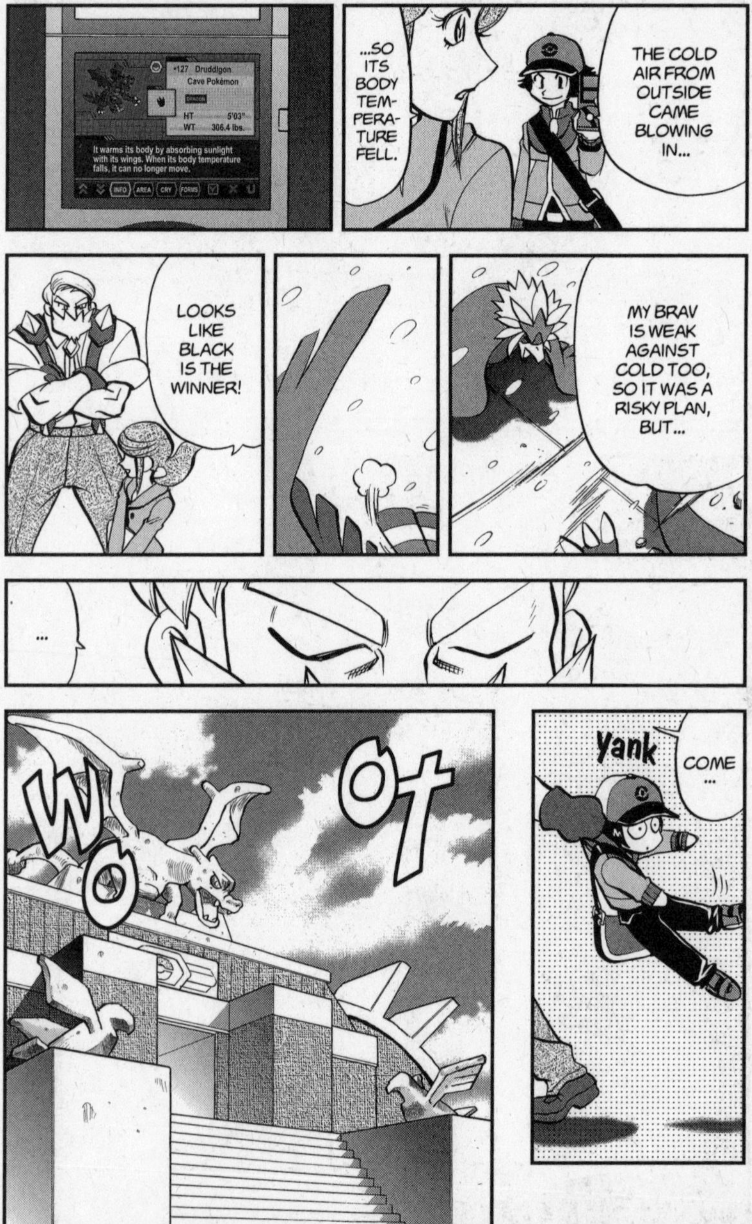
THE COLD AIR FROM OUTSIDE CAME BLOWING IN...
...SO ITS BODY TEM-PERA-TURE FELL.
•127 Druddigon
Cave Pokémon
DRAGON
HT 5'03"
WT 306.4 lbs.
It warms its body by absorbing sunlight with its wings. When its body temperature falls, it can no longer move.
INFO AREA CRY FORMS
MY BRAV IS WEAK AGAINST COLD TOO, SO IT WAS A RISKY PLAN, BUT...
LOOKS LIKE BLACK IS THE WINNER!
...
Yank
COME ...

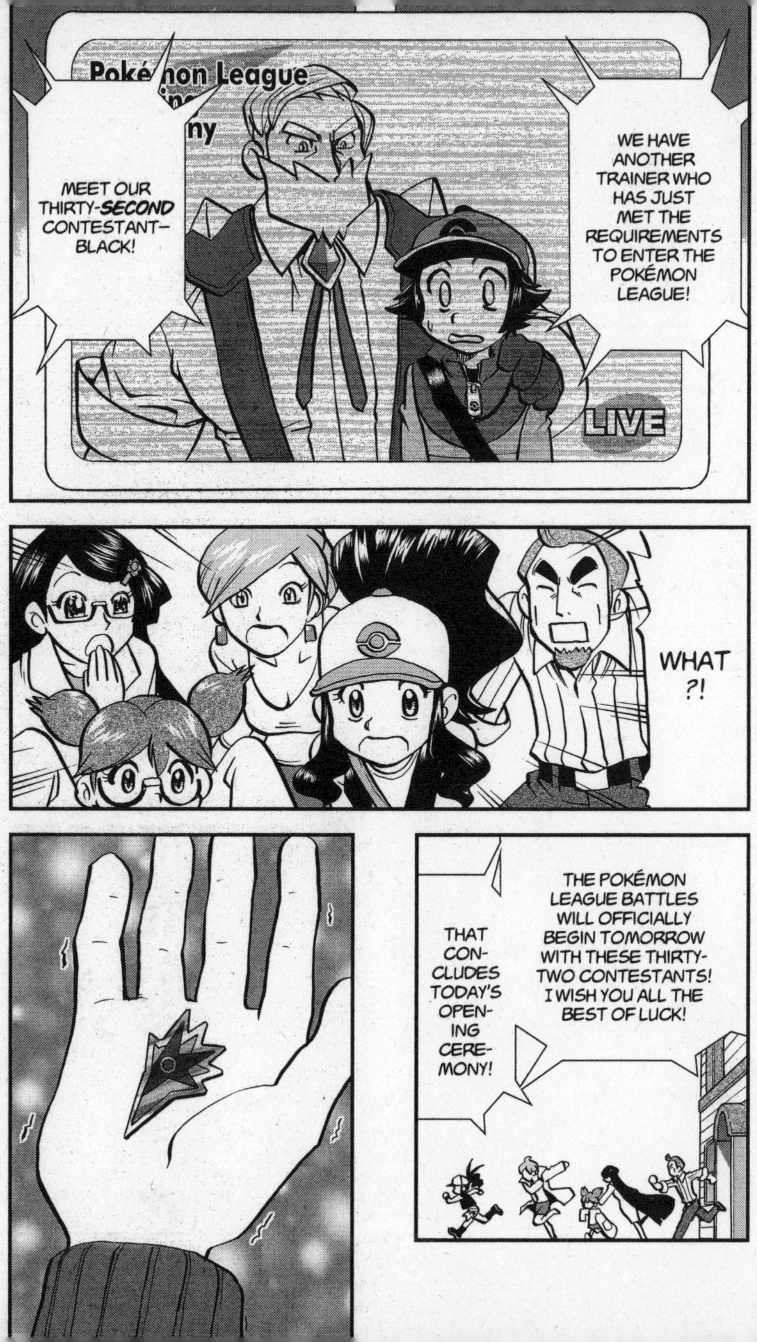
Pokémon League
WE HAVE ANOTHER TRAINER WHO HAS JUST MET THE REQUIREMENTS TO ENTER THE POKÉMON LEAGUE!
MEET OUR THIRTY-SECOND CONTESTANT—BLACK!
LIVE
WHAT?!
THE POKÉMON LEAGUE BATTLES WILL OFFICIALLY BEGIN TOMORROW WITH THESE THIRTY-TWO CONTESTANTS! I WISH YOU ALL THE BEST OF LUCK!
THAT CONCLUDES TODAY'S OPENING CEREMONY!

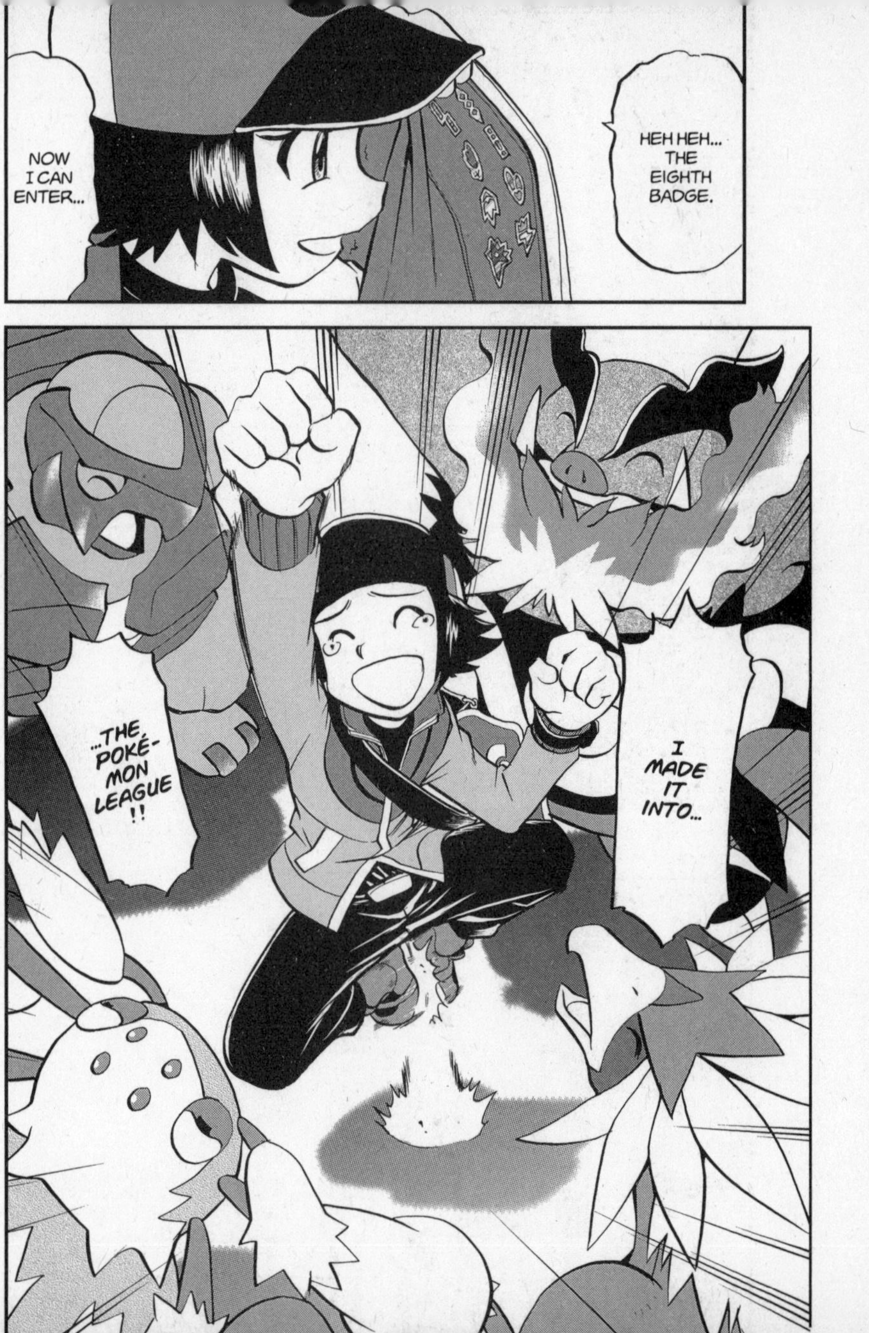
HEH HEH... THE EIGHTH BADGE.
NOW I CAN ENTER...
I MADE IT INTO...
...THE POKÉMON LEAGUE!!

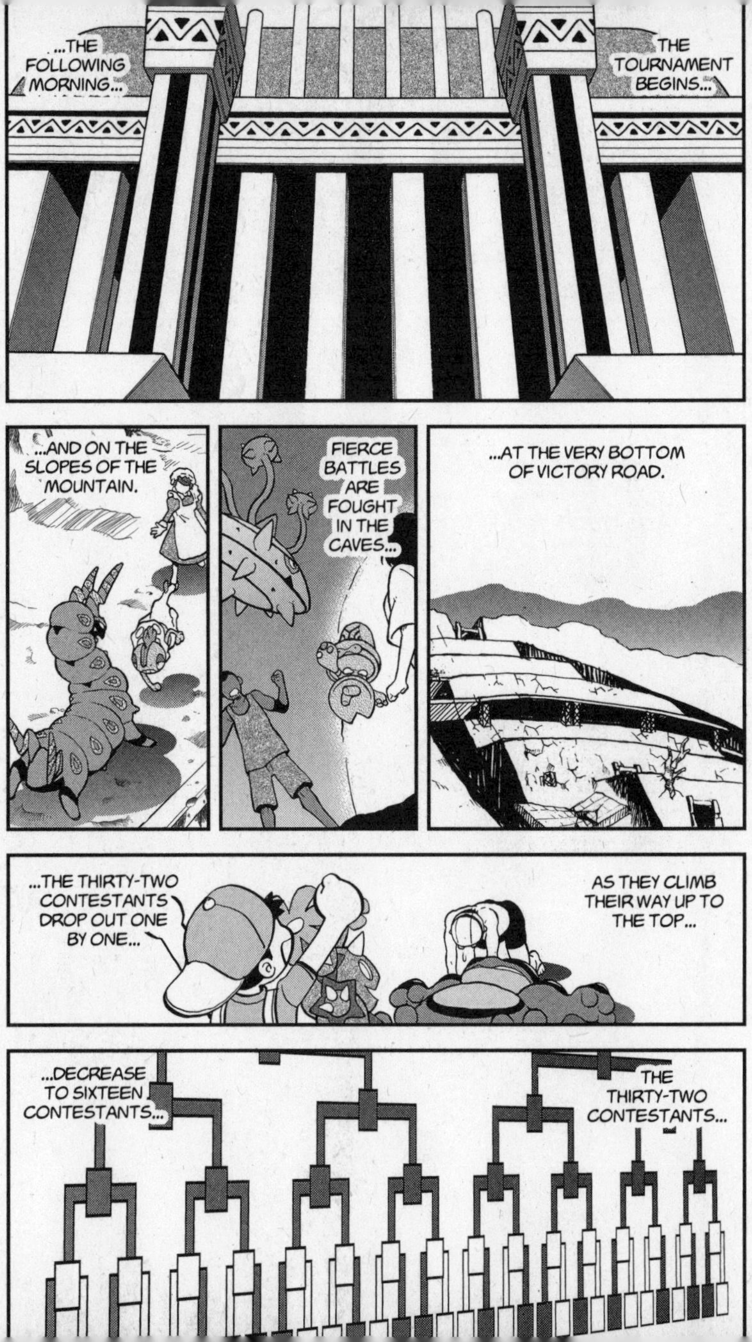
THE TOURNAMENT BEGINS...
...THE FOLLOWING MORNING...
...AT THE VERY BOTTOM OF VICTORY ROAD.
FIERCE BATTLES ARE FOUGHT IN THE CAVES...
...AND ON THE SLOPES OF THE MOUNTAIN.
AS THEY CLIMB THEIR WAY UP TO THE TOP...
...THE THIRTY-TWO CONTESTANTS DROP OUT ONE BY ONE...
THE THIRTY-TWO CONTESTANTS...
...DECREASE TO SIXTEEN CONTESTANTS...

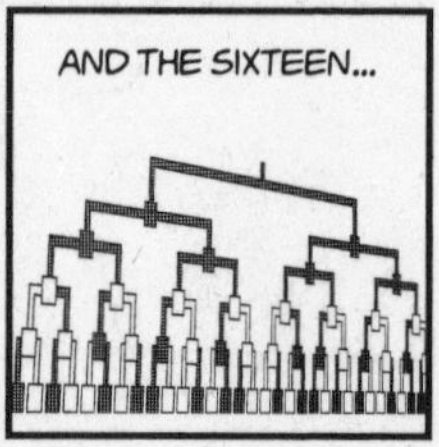
AND THE SIXTEEN...

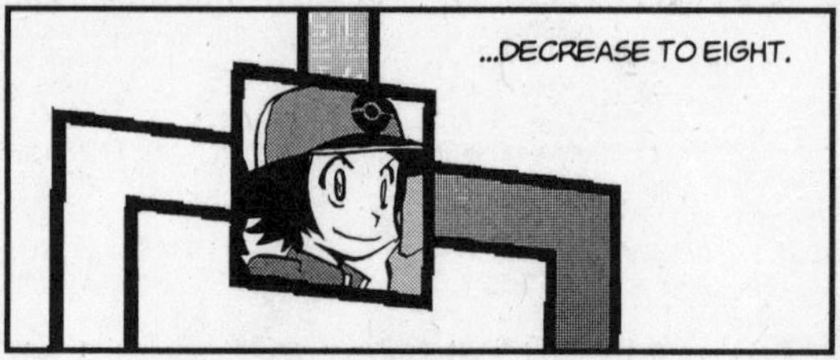
...DECREASE TO EIGHT.

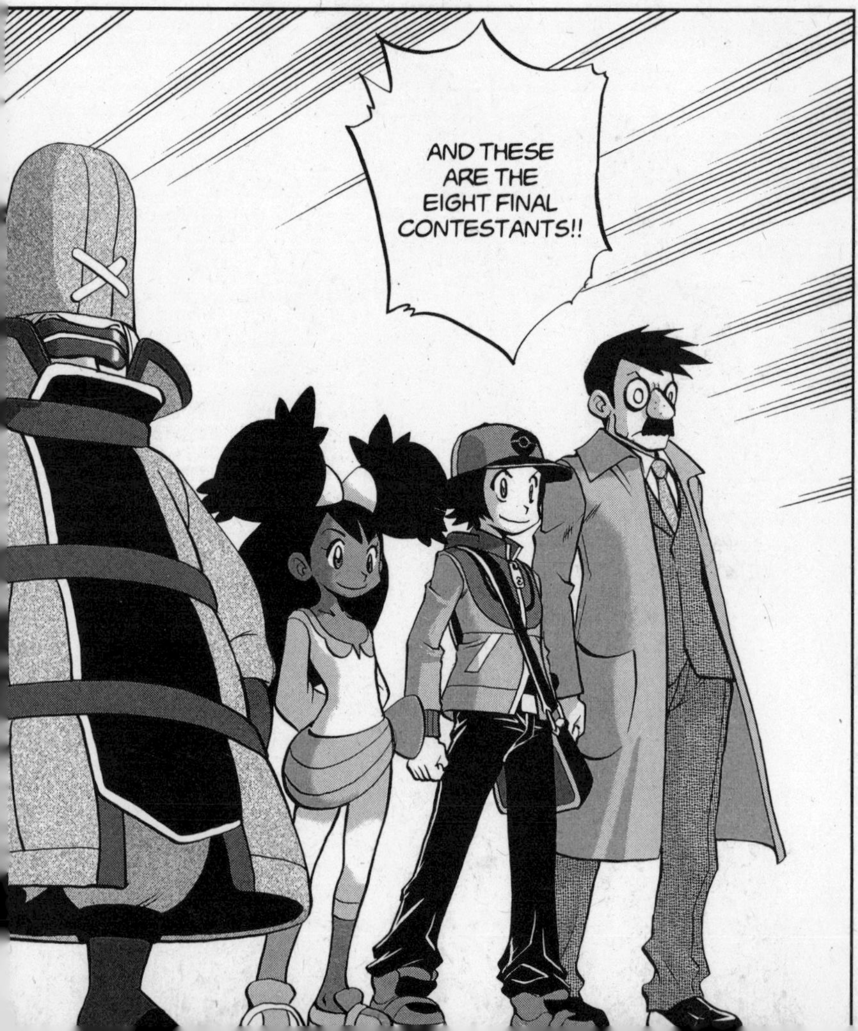
AND THESE ARE THE EIGHT FINAL CONTESTANTS!!

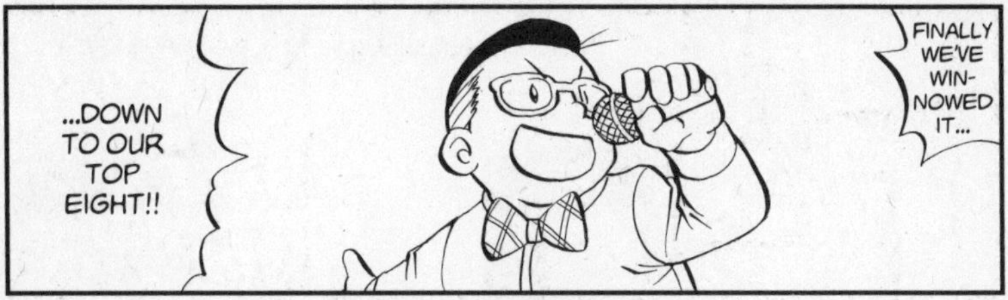
FINALLY WE'VE WIN-NOWED IT...
...DOWN TO OUR TOP EIGHT!!
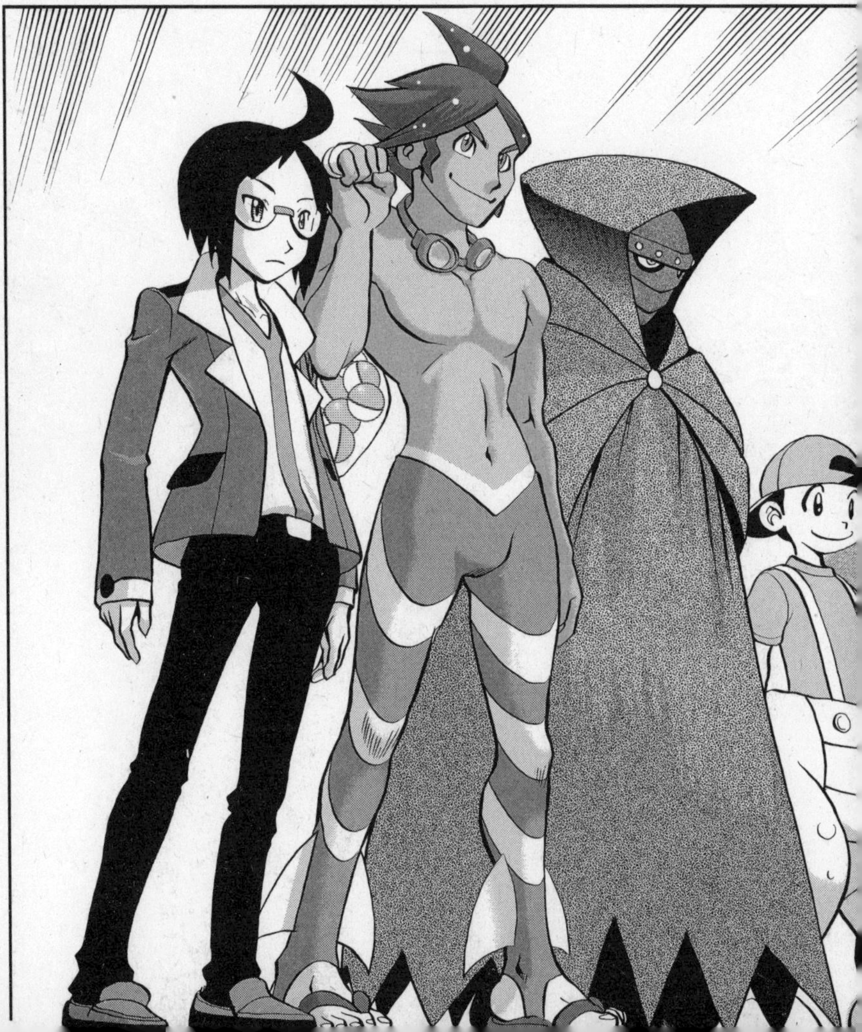

More Adventures COMING SOON...

...WHAT WE'RE FIGHTING FOR!

REMEMBER...

Black makes it to the quarter finals of the Pokémon League! But some of his opponents seem not only mysterious but downright suspicious... Then, he must battle Iris, who turns out to be a tougher opponent than he expected. Meanwhile, Cheren seems to have turned into a jerk!

HOW WILL BLACK SET CHEREN STRAIGHT...?

Plus, meet Deino, Jellicent, Beheeyem, Boldore, Fraxure and Haxorus!

VOL. 17 AVAILABLE AUGUST 2014!

POKÉMON
BLACK & WHITE

STORY & ART BY **SANTA HARUKAZE**

YOUR FAVORITE POKÉMON FROM THE UNOVA REGION LIKE YOU'VE NEVER SEEN THEM BEFORE!

Available now!

A pocket-sized book brick jam-packed with four-panel comic strips featuring all the Pokémon Black and White characters, Pokémon vital statistics, trivia, puzzles, and fun quizzes!

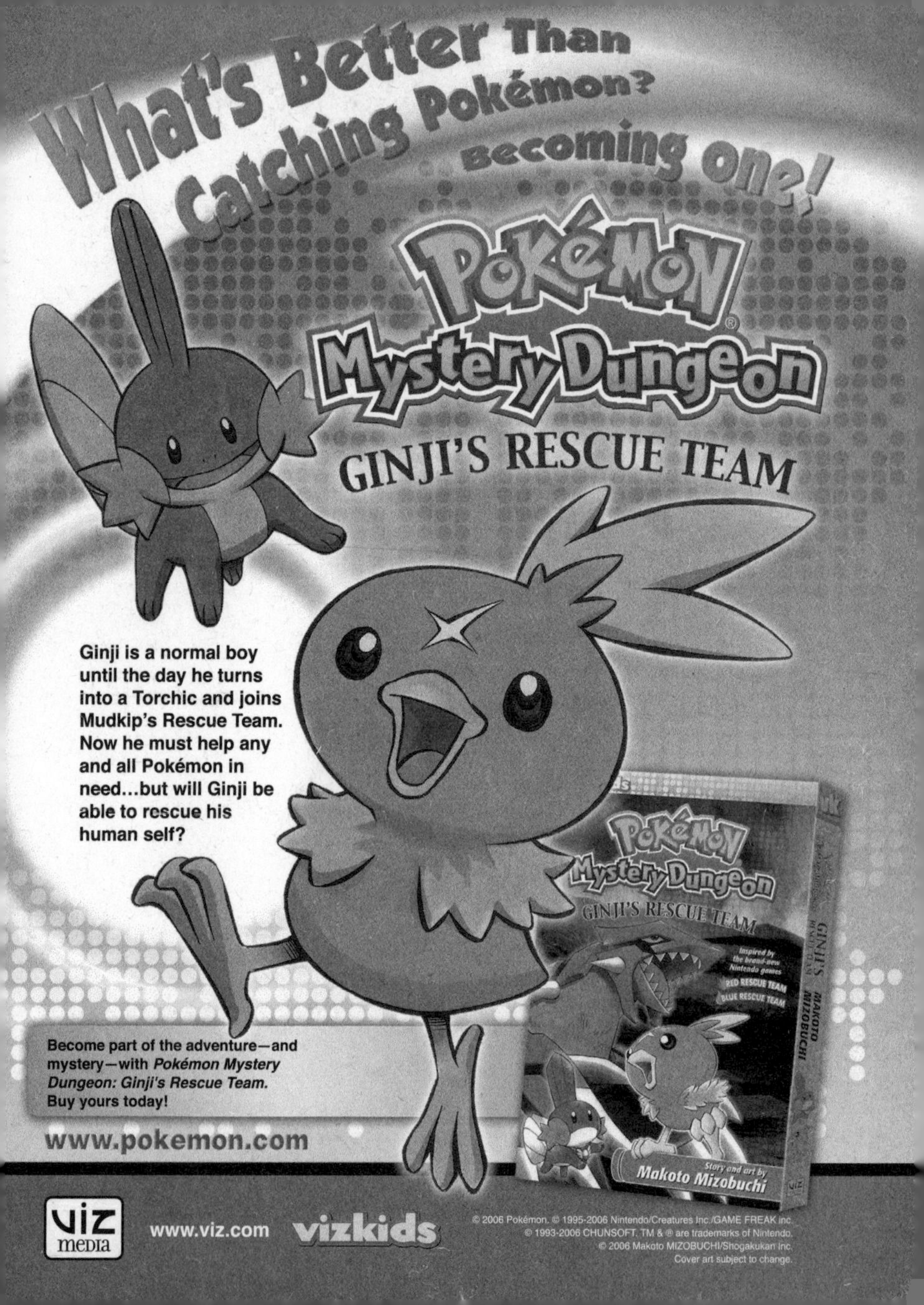
What's Better Than Catching Pokémon?
Becoming one!
POKÉMON® Mystery Dungeon
GINJI'S RESCUE TEAM
Ginji is a normal boy until the day he turns into a Torchic and joins Mudkip's Rescue Team. Now he must help any and all Pokémon in need...but will Ginji be able to rescue his human self?
Pokémon Mystery Dungeon
GINJI'S RESCUE TEAM
Inspired by the brand-new Nintendo games
RED RESCUE TEAM
BLUE RESCUE TEAM
GINJI'S RESCUE TEAM
MAKOTO MIZOBUCHI
Story and art by
Makoto Mizobuchi
Become part of the adventure—and mystery—with *Pokémon Mystery Dungeon: Ginji's Rescue Team.* Buy yours today!
www.pokemon.com
VIZ media
www.viz.com
vizkids
© 2006 Pokémon. © 1995-2006 Nintendo/Creatures Inc./GAME FREAK inc.
© 1993-2006 CHUNSOFT. TM & ® are trademarks of Nintendo.
© 2006 Makoto MIZOBUCHI/Shogakukan Inc.
Cover art subject to change.

vizkids
Pokémon
ARCEUS
AND THE
JEWEL OF LIFE
Story and Art by
Makoto Mizobuchi
Original Concept by Satoshi Tajiri
Supervised by Tsunekazu Ishihara
Script by Hideki Sonoda

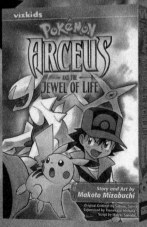

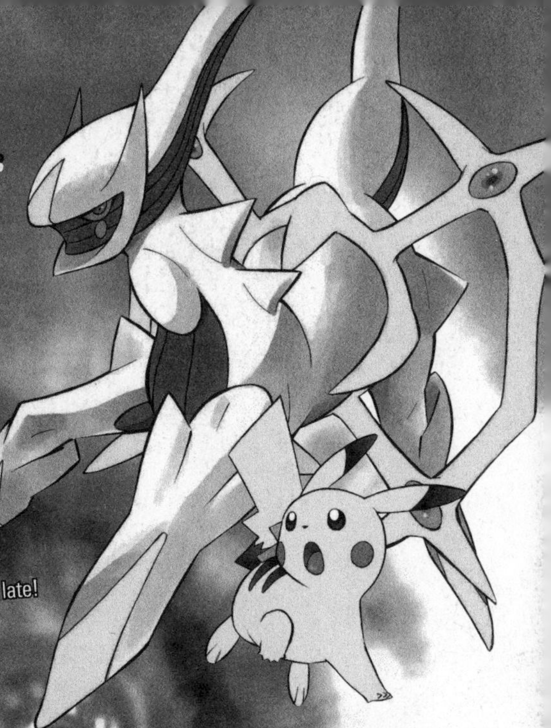

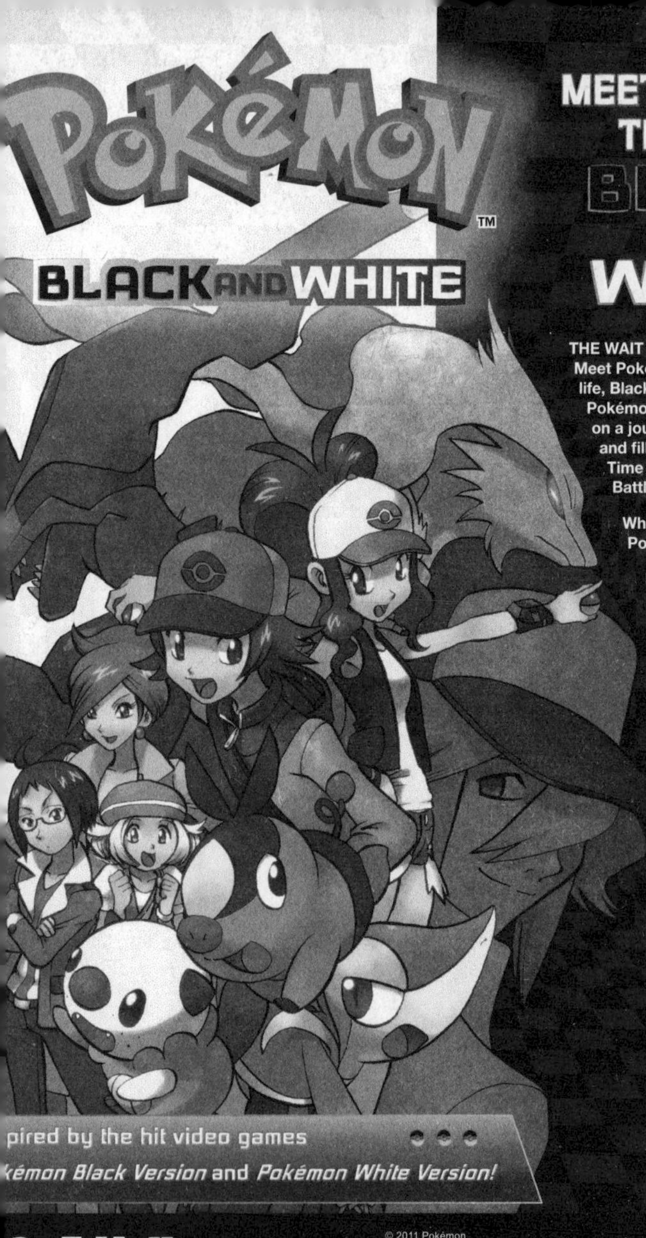

POKÉMON™
BLACK AND WHITE
pired by the hit video games
kémon Black Version and Pokémon White Version!

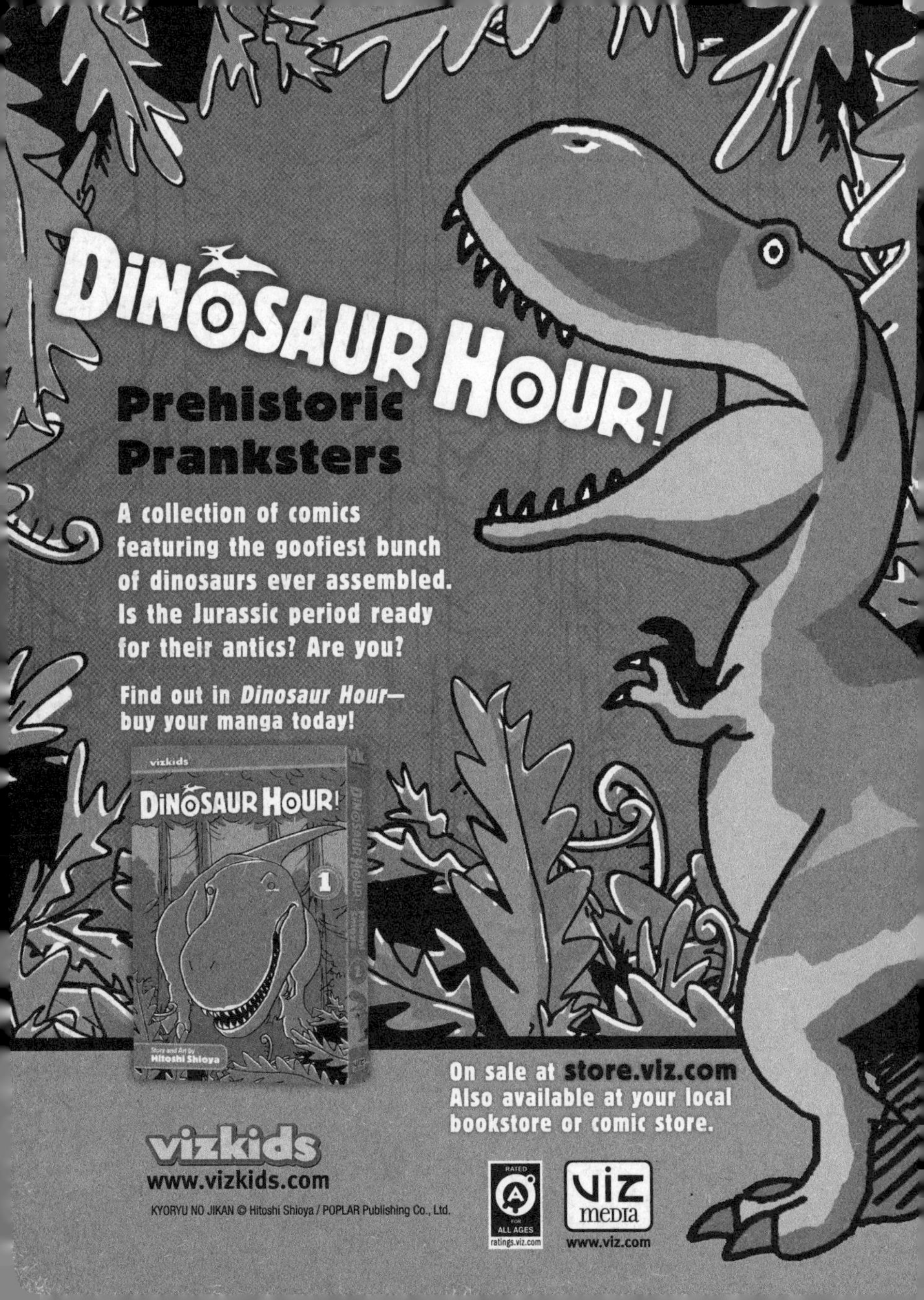
DINOSAUR HOUR!
Prehistoric Pranksters
A collection of comics featuring the goofiest bunch of dinosaurs ever assembled. Is the Jurassic period ready for their antics? Are you?
Find out in Dinosaur Hour—buy your manga today!
vizkids
DINOSAUR HOUR!
1
Story and Art by Hitoshi Shioya
On sale at store.viz.com
Also available at your local bookstore or comic store.
vizkids
www.vizkids.com
KYORYU NO JIKAN © Hitoshi Shioya / POPLAR Publishing Co., Ltd.
RATED A FOR ALL AGES
ratings.viz.com
VIZ MEDIA
www.viz.com

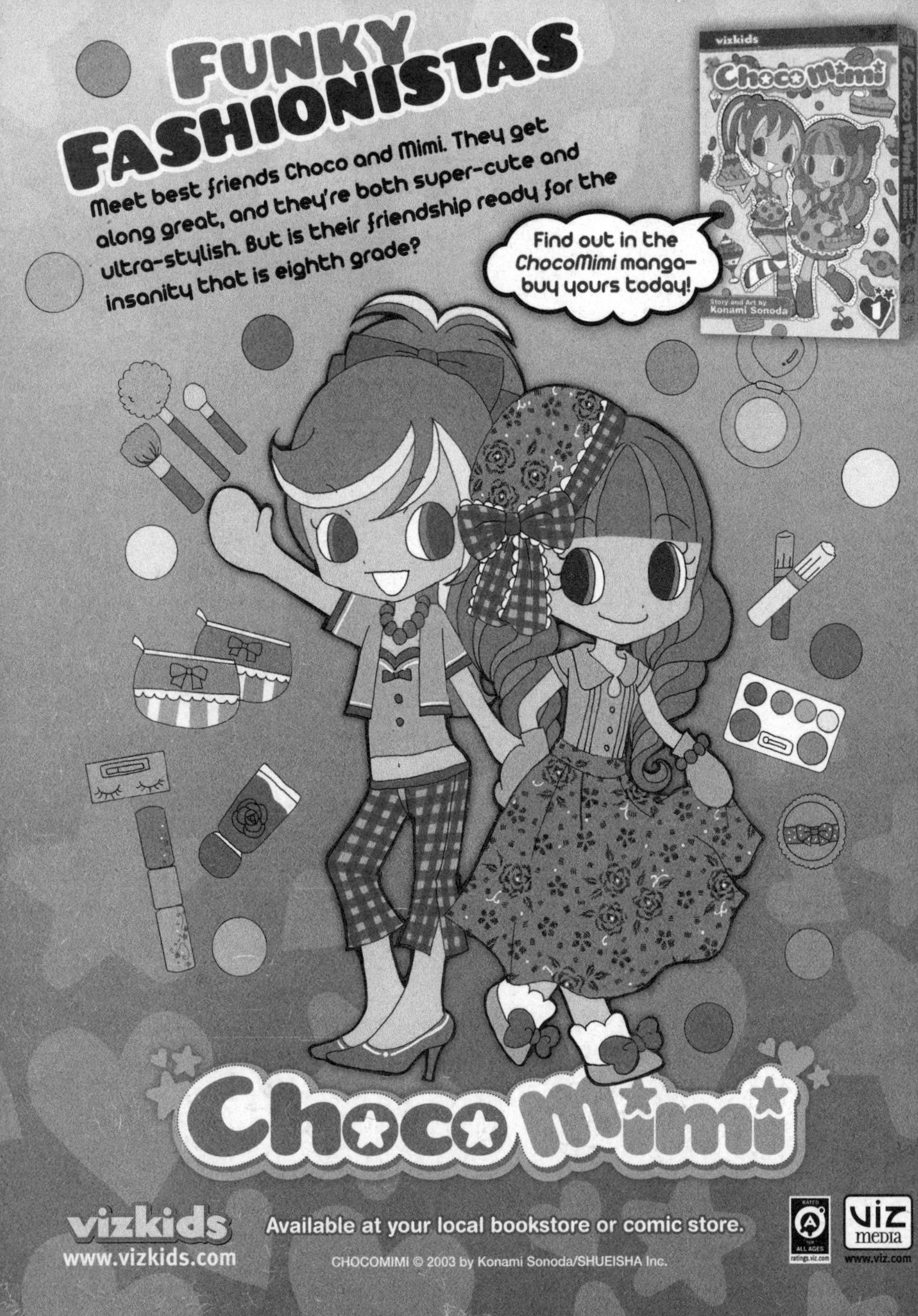
FUNKY FASHIONISTAS
Meet best friends Choco and Mimi. They get along great, and they're both super-cute and ultra-stylish. But is their friendship ready for the insanity that is eighth grade?
Find out in the ChocoMimi manga–buy yours today!
vizkids
ChocoMimi
Story and Art by Konami Sonoda
ChocoMimi
vizkids
www.vizkids.com
Available at your local bookstore or comic store.
CHOCOMIMI © 2003 by Konami Sonoda/SHUEISHA Inc.
ALL AGES
ratings.viz.com
VIZ media
www.viz.com

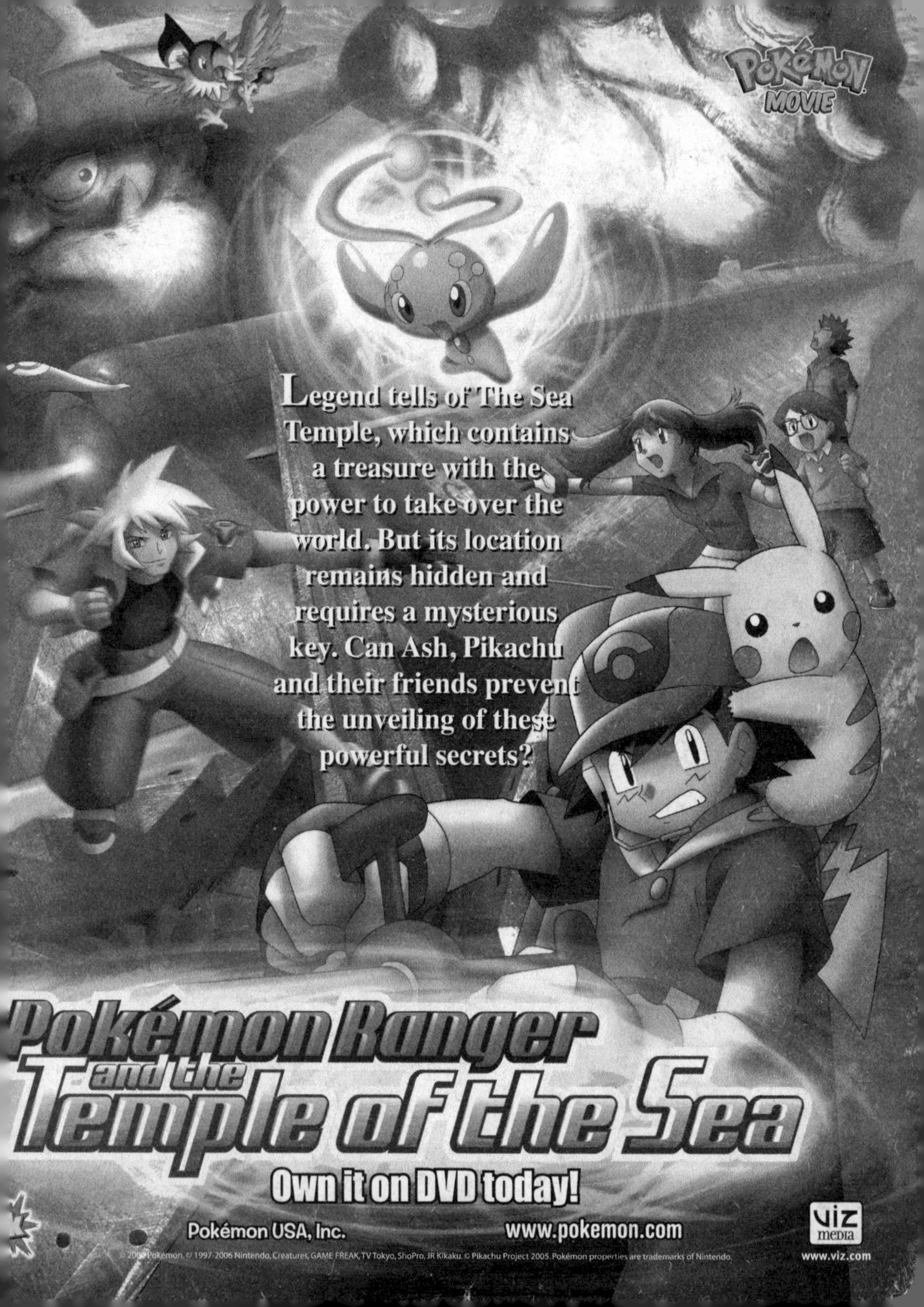

Pokémon MOVIE
Legend tells of The Sea Temple, which contains a treasure with the power to take over the world. But its location remains hidden and requires a mysterious key. Can Ash, Pikachu and their friends prevent the unveiling of these powerful secrets?
Pokémon Ranger and the Temple of the Sea
Own it on DVD today!
Pokémon USA, Inc.
www.pokemon.com
viz media
© 2006 Pokémon. © 1997-2006 Nintendo, Creatures, GAME FREAK, TV Tokyo, ShoPro, JR Kikaku. © Pikachu Project 2005. Pokémon properties are trademarks of Nintendo.
www.viz.com

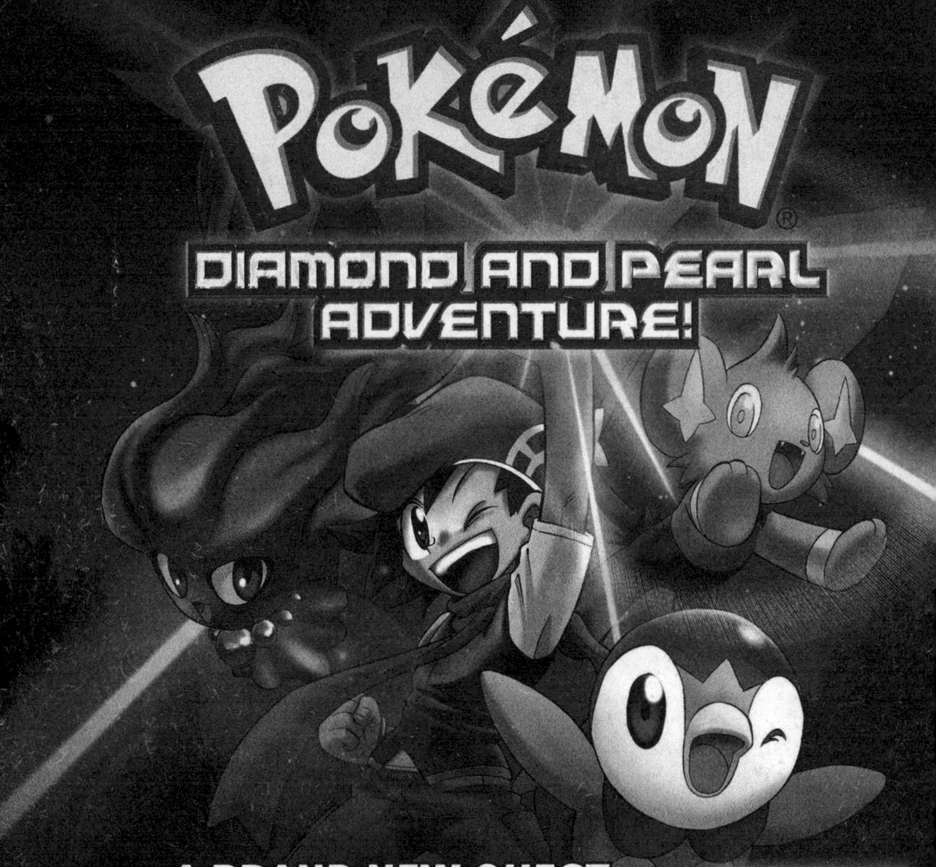
POKÉMON®
DIAMOND AND PEARL
ADVENTURE!

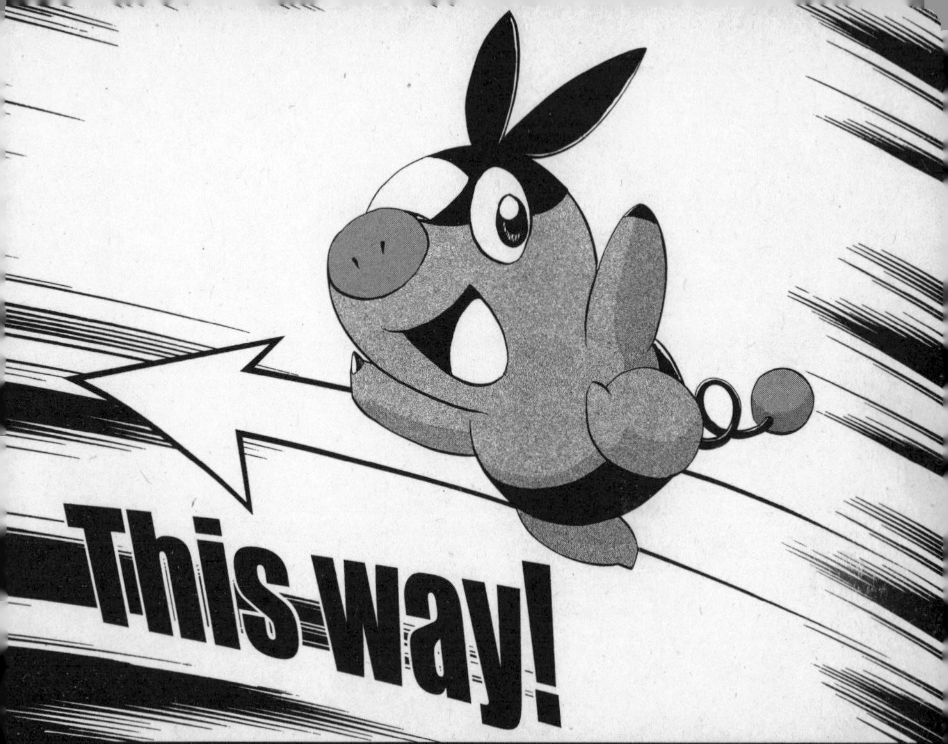
This way!

THIS IS THE END OF THIS GRAPHIC NOVEL!

To properly enjoy this VIZ Media graphic novel, please turn it around and begin reading from right to left.

This book has been printed in the original Japanese format in order to preserve the orientation of the original artwork. Have fun with it!

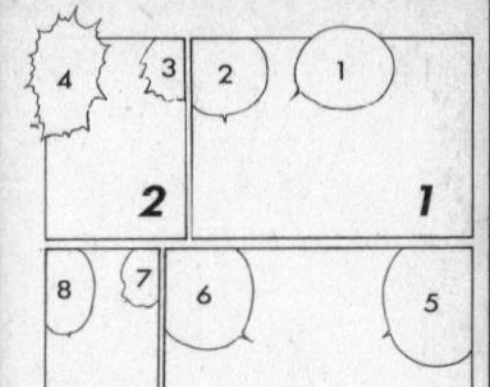
1
2
3
4
5
6
7
8
9
1
2
3
4
5

follow the action this way.